Entrapment . . .

"Don't make a move." Phelps stepped out from behind the house-sized rock with a gun in his hand. "Well, if it ain't Slocum and Bob."

The only other sound Slocum heard was the spill of water over the small falls. His heart sunk. How had he walked into such a trap?

"Stand there," Phelps said, and slipped around, taking her gun first. Then, with it in his waistband, he slipped behind Slocum.

Time to take action. He drove his elbow backward and threw Phelps off balance. Then Slocum whirled and caught the barrel of Phelps's six-gun and drove it skyward.

He drove his fist into Phelps's midsection, and the outlaw gasped for breath . . .

JAKE LOGAN

SLOCUM
AND THE
RANCHER'S DAUGHTER

JOVE BOOKS, NEW YORK

THE BERKLEY PUBLISHING GROUP
Published by the Penguin Group
Penguin Group (USA) Inc.
375 Hudson Street, New York, New York 10014, USA
Penguin Group (Canada), 90 Eglinton Avenue East, Suite 700, Toronto, Ontario M4P 2Y3, Canada
(a division of Pearson Penguin Canada Inc.)
Penguin Books Ltd., 80 Strand, London WC2R 0RL, England
Penguin Group Ireland, 25 St. Stephen's Green, Dublin 2, Ireland (a division of Penguin Books Ltd.)
Penguin Group (Australia), 250 Camberwell Road, Camberwell, Victoria 3124, Australia
(a division of Pearson Australia Group Pty. Ltd.)
Penguin Books India Pvt. Ltd., 11 Community Centre, Panchsheel Park, New Delhi—110 017, India
Penguin Group (NZ), 67 Apollo Drive, Rosedale, North Shore 0632, New Zealand
(a division of Pearson New Zealand Ltd.)
Penguin Books (South Africa) (Pty.) Ltd., 24 Sturdee Avenue, Rosebank, Johannesburg 2196,
South Africa

Penguin Books Ltd., Registered Offices: 80 Strand, London WC2R 0RL, England

This is a work of fiction. Names, characters, places, and incidents either are the product of the author's imagination or are used fictitiously, and any resemblance to actual persons, living or dead, business establishments, events, or locales is entirely coincidental.

SLOCUM AND THE RANCHER'S DAUGHTER

A Jove Book / published by arrangement with the author

PRINTING HISTORY
Jove edition / November 2008

Copyright © 2008 by Penguin Group (USA) Inc.
Cover illustration by Sergio Giovine.

ISBN: 978-0-515-14545-8

JOVE®
Jove Books are published by The Berkley Publishing Group,
a division of Penguin Group (USA) Inc.
375 Hudson Street, New York, New York 10014.
JOVE® is a registered trademark of Penguin Group (USA) Inc.
The "J" design is a trademark belonging to Penguin Group (USA) Inc.

PRINTED IN THE UNITED STATES OF AMERICA

10 9 8 7 6 5 4 3 2 1

Prologue

In leg irons and handcuffs, the three prisoners walked stiffly out of the courthouse into the glaring sun. A guard armed with a shotgun prodded them along. The woman's brother Searle never even looked in her direction. His head down in defeat, he climbed into the barred prison wagon, chained between the other two men.

There was no justice in Arizona Territory—least of all in the court system of Saguaro County. Searle hadn't stolen any horses. Those broncs with the blotched brands were planted on him by the man who owned them, Charles Worthington. Why would Searle steal WT horses anyway? He owned lots better horseflesh than Worthington's broomtails.

Maybe the governor up in Prescott would believe her. Trouble was she didn't dare leave their outfit for that long. No telling what would happen to the place the minute she turned her back—no, she'd have to write him a personal letter.

She was heartbroken as the driver and armed guard climbed on the seat of the prison wagon. With a shout, the wagon pulled out powered by four stout mules, leaving behind a cloud of dust.

Searle, I'll do all I can. I promise to hold the place together. With a cluck to the hip-shot team, she put a dusty boot on the dashboard and reared back on the spring seat to rein them around in a circle. It was time to stop feeling sorry for herself and get back to the ranch—there was lots to do. And with Searle gone, there was no one but her to work the place.

The notion made her sick to her stomach. She kept the cow ponies trotting with an occasional clucking or a slap on the butt with a line. The tireless horses were in good condition to hitch or ride. They were used for working cattle and driving. That was her late father's idea. An animal had to earn its keep or he got rid of it. Maybe if he was still alive he'd have gotten rid of her—for letting that two-bit sheriff Jesse Gantry and Worthington railroad her brother into Yuma Prison. Perhaps a better lawyer would have built a better defense. She slapped Curly on the hip with the rein for lagging a little. When he was back in stride, she nodded in approval. The heat waves distorted her vision of the distant purple hills. She wouldn't be home until near dark at the rate they were traveling through the rolling brown bunchgrass and cactus. Nothing would free her from the guilt she felt over her brother's conviction.

She'd never cried—not when they buried Pa—not when she'd had to shoot her favorite horse Scooter because he'd broken his leg in a bad fall. For sure she would not cry over this either—she'd get Searle out of prison—he was innocent. Starting to shake with fury, she sat up straight on the seat. It might be different if she'd ever been a little girl—she'd always been more boy than girl and she could run that ranch. She'd hold things together—for three years if she had to. That was her brother's sentence.

The setting sun was at her back when she drove the buckboard down off the last ridge. The windmill creaked loudly in the hot afternoon wind that swept her face as she urged the horses on for the last quarter mile. Under the tall rustling cottonwoods sat the low-walled adobe house with the shake roof, along with some sheds, haystacks, and corrals. Beyond were the golden-stubble fields of winter barley. With limited irrigation water and a winter rain or two, they'd managed to grow a small crop of winter grain for hay. The marginal water supply wasn't enough for any more crop production than that.

She swung the team in a semicircle to let the hot wind sweep the dust behind her away from the house and herself. When the reins were tied off, she bailed off the seat, and froze at the sight of the man.

He stood by the corral, sucking on a grass stem. With his back to the rails, he looked at her mildly. On his shirt, the deputy badge beaten out of a ten-centavo piece flashed in the sunset. From under the dusty black felt hat, some of his wavy black locks had escaped and stood out from his leathery tanned face. His dark eyes were like a wolf's as he looked her over like she was a bitch in heat. His mouth was a straight line without any mercy. He stepped out to intercept her, catching her arm.

She shrugged him off and stalked on by toward the house. A pain of deep regret knifed her—why did she leave the .44/40 in the buckboard? Because he was the law. The law didn't harm people. You didn't shoot lawmen.

He hurried after her and caught her arm, and she tried to twist away.

"Where're you going so fast, bitch?" he asked through his teeth, as he held on to her arm.

His viselike grip hurt, but she'd give him no pleasure by showing it. "Let go of me!"

"Not so fast. You don't have anyone around here that I can see to protect you." He acted like he was surveying the place. Then he jerked her up close to his mouth, which stank of sour whiskey. "You need a man."

"I damn sure don't need you, Claude Phelps."

"You need a man," he repeated, twisting her arm harder.

"Like hell I do." She drew back and hit him in the face with her doubled-up fist.

The blow jarred him enough that she slipped loose from his hold. She began to run hard for the house. Escape was her goal. As she looked back at Phelps, two powerful men came out of nowhere, one on each side, and caught her by the arms. A part-time deputy named Carson had her right arm, and another badge toter named Yodder had her left. The pain in her shoulders was excruciating as they forced her forward hard with their other hands, putting painful pressure on the sockets.

"All right," she said in surrender. Anything to get them to let up.

"Well?" Carson asked Phelps.

"Strip her clothes off and tie her on the bed. The fun's about to begin." His raw laughter echoed in her ears. He opened the door and they dragged her struggling inside the dark house.

The hopelessness of the situation roiled her guts enough to make her want to puke all over them. They were all lawmen. Deputy sheriffs . . .

Chapter 1

In the first light of dawn, he set the saddle on the ground and studied the ranch buildings and the stubble fields beyond them. His gritty eyes focused on the creaking windmill. Water. He could use some. The evening before, he'd had to put down his good horse who'd colicked, and he'd been on the move ever since to locate something to drink. Packing the saddle on his shoulder in the hope of finding another mount, he'd left his bedroll behind cached in a tree.

Surely, the rancher who owned this spread had a pony to sell or to loan him. If worse came to worst, he might get a ride in a buckboard to the nearest town. He was a man with few choices—being afoot in this desert country was dead serious. That was the reason he'd hiked all night under the stars.

He set the saddle down on the horn. It could stay right there till he needed it. He'd packed the double-rigged kac far enough. Rambling down the wagon tracks in his high-heel boots toward the house, he noted other tracks in the dust. Three riders had left there, and from the fresh horse apples, they had left recently. Maybe the owners had ridden out? No matter. He'd drink their water till they got back.

Then he heard flies buzzing, and stepped away from the wagon tracks to look for the source. The flies were feasting on a dead black-and-white cow dog that he found lying in the knee-high grass. The animal had been shot several times. Why would anyone shoot a dog like that? They sure must have wanted him dead.

At the stock tank he found a gourd dipper, and put it under the pipe's spout of water that the windmill pumped into the large tank. Sipping on the cool refreshment, he slaked his thirst. Not bad-tasting water in a land of gyp.

A horse snorted, and he saw a team hitched to a buckboard. They were pinned to the corral by the buckboard behind them. Why were they still harnessed? Out of habit, he shifted around the Colt on his hip.

He backed the horses out of their position and decided they needed a drink. Speaking softly to them, he began to unhitch them from the wagon. He bent over and unhooked the singletree from the horse on the right. Putting up the traces, he patted the first horse on the rump and slipped behind him to undo the other one. Then he went to take off the tongue.

He glanced at the house. There was no activity. Three riders had left there earlier, a shot-up stock dog lay beside the road, and a team had obviously been left hitched for a while. It didn't add up to much he could sort out.

The horses drank deep from the mossy tank and he felt they'd be all right. Neither acted too greedy. They were good stout bulldog horses that could scramble up a steep talus-strewn slope and down the other side.

"Don't move a muscle." The cold words made him freeze. "Who in the hell're you?"

"I'm afoot. Lost my horse last night and found these horses over there in a fix when I got here." He indicated the corral. "They needed a drink."

"Phelps leave you behind?"

"Ma'am, I came in here afoot. I ain't seen a soul since

early yesterday." He was anxious to catch sight of the female source of the voice, but his hands remained frozen and his back remained turned.

"Phelps left you."

"I don't know any Phelps and he sure never left me. My saddle is sitting a hundred yards up the road where I set it. Above where that dead dog is at."

"Dead dog?" Her gasp was loud enough that he spun around and saw her pale face. She stood about five-eight. She was dressed in a billowing long-tail nightshirt, and he could tell little about her figure. But her brown eyes drilled holes in him and she tried to swipe the short brunette hair back from her face with her gun hand.

"Yes, there's a black-and-white stock dog dead up there. He was all shot up."

"Those bastards—"

"You must have some tough enemies."

"I do. What's your name?" Her left eye was black and her cheek under it looked swollen. She'd came out second best in a fight, he figured.

"Slocum."

She nodded as if digesting it. "What do you do?"

He wiped his wet upper lip on his calloused palm. "I can do about anything. Grease that windmill for one thing." He motioned toward it.

Her eyes narrowed as if gauging him. "You looking for work?"

"I could use some."

"You might not want to work for a woman." She paused like she was waiting for his answer.

"It pays the same?"

"I guess. Thirty a month and food."

Slocum nodded and indicated the team. "Good. I'll just put them horses up."

"Yes—" Her gun pitched forward and slipped from her hand. Her knees buckled under the nightshirt, and he moved in to catch her as she started to fall. Holding her in his arms, he headed for the house.

She started coming around. "Put—me—down."

He looked down into her bleary eyes and shook his head. "Take it easy. I'll put you on the bed."

"No!" she screamed, and began to fight him.

She fought like a furious hellcat, but he managed to stand her on her feet. But once she was out of his arms, her eyes flew shut and she wilted again. This time, he managed to deliver her to the rumpled bed. He wondered about the ropes on the head of the bed.

Stepping back, he waited for her to revive. What could he do for her?

Finally, half sitting up with one arm bracing herself, she swept the hair back from her face and looked at him as if she'd faint again. "Who're you?"

"Slocum."

"No, I mean who are you?"

"Just a fella drifting through. You want to tell me what's happened here?"

She rubbed the tops of her legs under the nightshirt. "I got taught a lesson here last night."

"What lesson?"

"Oh, what the hell. Three of Saguaro County's finest deputies raped me last night in this bed."

"They did what?" Slocum narrowed his eyes.

"I'm not going to repeat it."

"Three deputies—the three that rode off earlier?"

"You saw them?"

"I read their tracks. I've done some scouting."

She dropped back, using her hands behind her for support. "The prison wagon took my brother Searle to Yuma Prison yesterday. When I got home, they were waiting here like buzzards. Claude Phelps, Yodder, and Carson." She exhaled and scooted for the edge of the bed. "There's no sense crying over spilt milk. You put the horses in the corral. I'll fix us some breakfast."

With a nod, he started for the door and then he paused. "I never caught your name."

"Bob. That's short for Roberta."

"All right, Bob."

"There should be hay in that manger for them. You can see if it's there."

"I'll check."

"You like scrambled eggs?"

"I'd eat them any way but raw."

"Good." She waved him on.

He stood outside and looked at the hillside bathed in the morning light. Maybe in time she'd tell him the rest. Sounded like she'd been through a tough ordeal. He swept up her pistol from the dust and jammed it in his waistband. To give her some time to recover, he took his own time unharnessing the horses and putting them in the corral. Then he heard her ringing a handheld schoolhouse bell.

Better go eat. His belly button was glued to his backbone. He washed up on the porch setup, dried his hands on the Minnesota Pride flour-sack towel, and went inside. He put his hat on a peg and turned to look at Roberta dressed in a riding skirt and a man's collarless shirt. Her willowy figure made him realize she was an attractive young lady.

"Well, haven't you ever seen a woman before?" She held a skillet in each hand and motioned for him to go to the table. "Sit down. We can eat."

He took a seat, and she put the two cast-iron frying pans on the table. One was full of scrambled eggs and ham cut up. The other contained her brown-topped biscuits.

"That going to be enough?"

Looking at all the food, he shook his head. "I can't eat half of that."

"Better build your appetite. Three fourths of that is yours, mister."

Through the meal, she told him about her brother Searle's arrest and the unfair trial and his sentencing.

When she finished, he paused with half a biscuit in his hand and looked over at her. "You've had a world of hell around here."

She nodded. "You don't know the half of it."

"Them three threaten to come back?"

"If they do—" She clenched the fork handle in her fist and beat it on the table. "I'll kill 'em."

He rose in his chair, ready to go for a towel to sop up the coffee that had sloshed out of their cups. But she waved him down. "I'll get a rag."

Seated again, he watched her mop up the liquid. She turned and looked hard at him—her left eye was nearly swollen shut. "You afraid of them?" she asked.

"No."

Then she straightened and wadded the rag in her hands. "You don't look or act like a man who backs up from much."

"I just wanted to know the cards I have and what to expect."

She tossed the rag on the dry sink and sat down. "Yes, I figure they'll come back again. Next time I'll be ready. Next time . . ."

Tears began to roll down her cheeks and, sobbing, she rushed for the open door. "There won't be a next time."

He cradled the cup in his hand and studied the neat small kitchen. This was not the right moment to physically comfort her. She needed the time alone, but with her outside and crying, it made his belly hurt not to be able to do something. He went and squatted on his boot heels in the doorway.

The cool morning breeze swept his face. The Gambrel's quail called from out in the chaparral. On the bench to his right, she sobbed in her hands.

"I never cry . . ."

He nodded. "Sometimes things get so bad it's the only way out."

"You said those bastards killed Ring?" she asked. "The dog?"

"Yes. He's up the hill about fifty yards."

"I must bury him."

"I can do that—later." He sipped on the rich coffee. Those three needed a real lesson. He wasn't sure how to do it, but in his book they needed it.

"How well do you know this Phelps?" he asked.

"Know him? Before last night, I'd danced once or twice with him at community functions. Why do you ask?"

"Did he ever make any advances to you before yesterday?"

"Are you saying did I encourage him?"

"No. I was wondering if he'd planned on doing it."

"I'm not sure what you are getting at."

He shifted his weight to his other leg and glanced over at her. "I think you scorned his advances one time too many and yesterday was payback."

"Payback?" Behind her wet eyes, she cut an angry look at him.

"Hold on. I didn't say you encouraged him, but by denying him sometime or other, you brought out another side of him."

"I never liked him. He's such a banty rooster."

"What about the other two?"

"That conniving pair—"

"Are you planning to press charges against them?"

"What good would that do? It's my word against them. They're the law. Besides—"

He nodded. "I need to borrow a horse this morning. I've got my saddle here and there's a bedroll I stashed on the trail after I put my horse down. He colicked and twisted a gut, I guess. Nothing else I could do."

"I'm sorry. Go ahead. Either one of those horses you put up rides fine."

"You're going to be all right?"

"I guess so." She blinked at him like she couldn't believe he'd even ask. Maybe no one had ever asked her that before.

"Leave burying the dog to me," he said. "I'll be back in a couple of hours."

"Slocum—thanks."

"Sure." And he left her to get the pony and his saddle.

Two hours later, still backtracking himself, Slocum dropped off a ridge and smelled a fire. The scent came from a side canyon, and he decided to skirt it and try to see the source from the rim. Smoke in the middle of the morning usually meant a branding fire—it could be someone catching a late calf they'd missed, or it might be a rustler. Either way, he didn't intend to walk right up on a situation that could erupt into a shooting.

He left the pony hitched out of sight and started off the hillside under the cover of some large rocks. At last he drew close enough to understand the two men's words.

". . . heard that horse. Sooner we get this one branded, the better it will be."

"Quit worrying. We get this brand worked over, we can find a shady place and take a nap."

Worked over? Slocum drew his gun and kept close to the side of the house-sized rock. They needed to brand the critter before he could move in. He could barely hear them talking about the iron. He waited. And waited. Sweat trickled down from under arms. Then he finally heard the steer bawl.

He stepped out in time to see one of them standing over the critter with a running iron and the other getting up with the wet tow sack in his hand. They were too busy examining their work to know he was there.

"Don't do nothing fast," Slocum said with the six-gun in his hand.

"Huh?" They both whirled. Their hands flew into the air.

"Who in the hell are you?" the short swarthy one demanded.

The tall lanky one cut Slocum a tough look and said to his partner, "Keep your mouth shut. He ain't the law."

"You boys ever hear of vigilante law?"

"Yeah," Shorty said.

"That's the law I'm enforcing. Who do you boys work for?"

"We don't have to tell you nothing," Lanky said.

"That's right." Slocum took the guns out of their holsters and tossed them aside.

He glanced at the steer on the ground with his four legs tied. "Who owns that XA brand you just put on him?"

"Ain't none of your gawdamn business."

"I'm making it mine. Now get on your bellies, I'm tying you up."

"What in the hell're you going do to us?" Lanky asked.

Slocum didn't bother to answer them. He had the tall one's hands tied and was kneeling down beside him. "Now tell me your name or I'm using a running iron on your butt."

"Guy Dawson."

"And what's this other asshole's name?"

"Dun Manley."

"This ain't going to set well with some folks," Dawson said in a threatening tone.

"Who? Your boss?" He moved over to tie Manley.

"You'll see. You'll see."

When they were tied up, he went over to the steer lying on the ground, and tried to read the old brand on the two-year-old's side. It looked like a B7, but he couldn't tell with the new brand over it. There were B7 brands all over Roberta's place on the lumber and other places. AX made a good brand to put over it.

He better take the the two rustlers to this sheriff that she'd talked about. It would eat up a whole day. But there had to be a showdown with these people—her brother was gone and they were declaring open range on her body and livestock. She might not want to prosecute the rapist, but rustling was another thing.

He turned the steer loose. The two-year-old got up stiff, but not on the prod. Slocum waved the lariat he was coiling at him, and the steer spooked away. With a quick glance around, Slocum mentally marked the country he was in. If there was evidence needed for a trial, he might have to locate that critter again.

No telling what he'd stepped into—but with her brother gone, they damn sure had wasted no time moving in.

When the pair was loaded on the two cow ponies with the WT brands on their shoulders, he put leads on their mounts to bring them along. Then he climbed on Roberta's bay horse and headed back for the ranch.

It would be a lot of trouble to take the sullen-faced rustlers to the sheriff. Which was why the "lynch law" remained in effect and was still used frequently in the Southwest. He came over the hill to the ranch in a short lope. He saw Roberta step out of the shed and shade her eyes looking in his direction.

When he reined up, he noticed she'd strapped on the sidearm. She frowned at the men with their hands tied and sitting on the horses. "What happened?"

"These two were using a running iron on a B7 two-year-old. Put an AX on him."

"B7's my brand."

He nodded and stepped down. "You know them?"

"Yes, they work for Worthington. But you might as well turn them loose. The law won't do anything about them."

"Ma'am, we told him that," said Dawson.

Slocum turned on his heel and gave Dawson a look cold

enough to shut him up, then turned back to her. "We've got to start somewhere."

She nodded. "You want me to hitch the buckboard?"

"I can."

She checked the sun. "I better fix some lunch. It'll be dark by the time we get there."

"Fine," he said. "I'll unload them two and hitch the wagon."

"The chestnut with the white star and the sorrel with the white hind hoof are fresh. Hitch them. I can show you."

"No, you fix lunch. I can handle the rest."

She scowled at the pair and stalked off for the house. One at a time, he jerked the men off their horses. "I'm untying you two, but I'll shoot to kill if you try anything. Savvy?"

Both agreed. He undid the ropes, and they did lots of flexing of their hands and arms, then went inside the corral and emptied their bladders. He tossed them each a lead and ordered them to bring out the two horses she'd mentioned.

When they had the two ponies led out, he put the two men to currying them. He tossed the harness on the sorrel and motioned for Manley to buckle him up, then did the same on the chestnut with Dawson doing the job.

"You know you're making a big mistake taking us in," Dawson said when he finished. "You don't know who runs this county."

Slocum took the horse by the bridle and led him to the rig. "Maybe I'll learn who that is. Won't be my first mistake."

"I was just warning you."

"If you think I'm afraid, you better think again. I didn't come in here on a load of pumpkins."

"You don't know how things operate in these parts."

"Well, why don't you shut up or I'll retie you and gag your mouth."

Dawson shut up.

With the horses hitched, he herded the pair toward the house and told them to sit down on the porch. Roberta came to the door. "All I have are some beans."

"Put some on a couple of plates and they can eat out here."

Dawson took off his hat for her and started to say something. Slocum caught him by the shirt collar and jerked him back. "Sit down and shut up."

They sat down. She returned with two tins plates heaping with frijoles and with spoons to eat them. Both men thanked her.

Slocum washed up, dried his hands, and went inside. "Sorry, I know you didn't need this." He stood where he could see the men and still talk to her. "But we have to start someplace."

She dried her palms on the skirt and nodded. "There's just you and me. I'm sorry. I can pay you and give you a horse right now to ride on out of here. I don't know how this rustler thing will go. But that bunch runs this county and the courts."

"Time for a change."

"Searle thought so, too. Sam Lander did and they dry-gulched him."

"Well, we'll see."

She nodded and brought him a plate of beans. "I hate to involve you in all this."

"I've had worse deals handed me before. I'm just upset that you have to face them—those deputies. I imagine they'll be there in town."

"I have to live here. Sooner or later, my path will cross theirs anyway. I'll just have to face the fact."

He nodded sharply. She would have to do that. There was no way that he could protect her forever. At least he was there to help for the time being.

"You want some coffee?" she asked.

The sadness in her good brown eye looked deep. How

long had it been since they'd raped her? Not twenty-four hours. Damn, maybe this rustler business was going to be too tough on her. "Yes, I want the coffee. I'm sorry, my mind is on them two."

"I know. But I'm just not certain this is the way to handle it."

"We can lynch them," he said.

She shook her head at that notion, then swept the wave of light brown hair back from her face. "I'll set this coffee on a chair. Then you can stand here and watch them."

He said, "Fine." And saluted her with his spoonful of beans.

After lunch, he had her write out confessions for both of the men to sign. That they did use a running iron on a B7 steer, changing the brand to AX. That they also marked other range livestock in the same manner. That they were employed by Charles Worthington to do it.

Slocum made them both sit at the table. "Now you can sign this or if you don't, the last judge you will see is a cottonwood tree."

"You—you can't lynch us," Manley said, looking at Roberta for help.

"Slocum's the man. He says hang, you hang. Isn't that right?"

Slocum nodded in the silence.

"All right, I ain't hanging. But I'm probably signing my own damn death warrant." He dipped the pen and wrote his name on it.

Dawson did the same. When they were through, Slocum blew on the ink, then folded the papers and put them in his inside vest pocket. With a nod to Roberta standing with her arms folded in the doorway, he said to the pair, "Get in the rig. We're going to town."

Both men sat in the back of the buckboard as Roberta drove. Slocum rode a bald-faced horse. She'd told him it was her brother's favorite horse. He soon learned why. Baldy single-footed instead of trotted, which made for an easy ride as he brought the rustlers' two horses on leads— one on each side. Riding behind the rig, he kept a close watch on the two men.

They'd silenced up, but he still expected them to try something. It would be the last thing they ever did. No telling what would happen in town—he'd need to be ready for anything. How would she take it? No telling. He'd better enjoy his good horse. It was the only good thing that was going to happen to him this day.

Antelope Springs was close to a river with the same name. Save for some gnarled cottonwoods on the banks, the small stream of water that snaked down the sandy riverbed looked unimpressive when the buckboard rumbled over the wooden plank bridge. The town's buildings were of wood and adobe, and save for some freight wagons and teams of oxen, the place looked quiet in the late afternoon.

A few town dogs ran out to bark, but kept a respectable distance. Roberta reined up before the jail and he dismounted behind the rig.

"Get down," he said to the pair, and they scooted off the buckboard.

"Get inside." He motioned toward the adobe building.

A tall man stood in the doorway. Curly black hair framed his face. He looked about thirty years old, with hard eyes and a tough jaw. For an instant, Slocum wondered where he knew the man from—somewhere in the past—him or a man just like him. The man stood like a barrier and nodded to the two men before he spoke. "What have we got here?"

"Two rustlers."

"You the law?" The man looked past them at Slocum.

"I take it you are."

"Damn right I'm the law. What're you going to do about it?"

"Lock them up. I'm signing a warrant for their arrest for rustling."

Unmoved, the deputy laughed. "You ain't even a registered voter."

"Nope. Are you going to stand there with your thumb in your ass all day or do something?"

"Listen, mister." The deputy started from the door—

The metallic click of a cartridge being levered into a rifle chamber stopped him.

"That's far enough, Phelps," Roberta said. "He's my man and he caught those two working over a brand on one of my steers. Now get in there and do your job."

"Listen—"

"Move," she ordered, and drew the rifle up to her shoulder.

"You two are going to regret this."

Phelps went inside. Slocum hustled the pair in after him. He nodded toward the open cell and they went in— Manley protesting. "I told him. I told him. He couldn't arrest us."

"Yeah, he ain't got no right—"

"Shut up," Phelps said to Dawson, and frowned hard at the two to quiet them as he closed the cell door.

"Here, better lock them in there." Slocum tossed Phelps the keys on a big ring he took from the paper-cluttered desk, and Phelps caught them, but not without an angry look.

"I'll sign the warrant," she said. "I'm a taxpayer."

"You know having a trial costs this county big bucks."

"Cost never bothered you when you arrested Searle." She set the rifle across the top of the desk and looked for something. At last, she found the paper and dipped the pen in the inkwell and wrote her name, Roberta Bakker, in the appropriate place, and then wrote that Guy Dawson and Dun Manley were caught red-handed using a running iron on a steer with a B7 brand on it, changing it to an AX, on August 15, 1878.

She signed it and had Slocum sign it, too. "That should hold them for the judge."

Phelps shook his head. "You two are wasting your time. What court of law's going to believe a horse thief's sister and some saddle tramp?"

She whipped the rifle up and Slocum caught the barrel to stop her. "Phelps, you may have nine lives, but you just used up one of them," he said.

A pin falling would have been loud. Slocum then nodded at the door, and for moment he felt that she was getting ready to twist the rifle from his hand—it passed and she went on outside.

"Now when's the circuit judge due in here?" Slocum asked.

"Depends. Month, six weeks."

"Maybe the governor could send one sooner. So them boys don't have to fret too long in jail here before they get sentenced."

"Mister, I don't know who the hell you are, but you go to messing with the law here, you'll be buzzard bait."

"Don't ever come back to the B7 with a hard-on again. You'll come home a gelding."

"Yeah?"

Slocum nodded. "Oh, your prisoners may need supper."

"Get the hell out of here," Phelps raged.

Slocum nodded and turned to go outside to join her at the buckboard. Phelps would be a tough one. But he would crumble before this was over. Slocum owed it to Roberta to be sure Phelps was fully paid back.

With a wary shake of her head as she looked at the lighted doorway of the jail, she said, "Let's get some supper and then we can drive back to the ranch."

He agreed and unhitched Baldy from the rack. On foot, he followed her and the rig down the empty darkening street to the café. One day in this country and he was already in a mess. Maybe he looked for tough situations like this, or maybe they drew him in.

Shame that Phelps and his two buddies weren't sharing that cell. Damn shame.

Chapter 2

He reached past Roberta and opened the door. The café was hot, and the rich smell of cooking filled the air. Faces turned, and some customers blinked at the sight of the two of them. Roberta led him to a table and indicated the opposite chair.

"We naked?" he asked under his breath as he sat down across from her.

"Naked?"

"They looked us over like we were."

"They're not used to me showing up with a man. Especially a stranger."

"Evening, Roberta." An older gentleman removed his hat and stopped before their table.

"Sam Lowery, good to see you. This is my new hired hand, Slocum."

Sam extended a hand and they shook.

"Take care of her," he said. "She's been through a lot. If I can help, let me know."

"I will," Slocum said. If that man behind the white handlebar only knew the half of it.

"Well, I've got to get back and check on the stock. Good to meet you."

"Sam?" she said. He stopped. "Slocum and I brought in two of Worthington's men on rustling charges. Slocum caught them working over a brand on one of my steers."

He shook his head gravely. "It'll only make him madder."

"I know, but I felt I needed to do something."

"There ain't no end to it. Times I want to give up and sell out." He rested his gnarled hands on the top of the chair. "If I was thirty . . . but I ain't."

"There has to be justice somewhere, Sam."

"Not in this county. See you," Sam said to both of them, and turned to leave.

Slocum watched his retreat to the front door. His slightly bent posture and the limp in his walk showed the mark of the man's years. He'd do as a friend.

When he went outside, Roberta looked at Slocum. "He's a good man."

"Sorry, folks," the rawboned, red-faced woman said, wiping her hands on her apron. "My help's sick. I'm working shorthanded. What can I get you? Heavens to Betsy, what happened to you, girl?"

"It's long story, I'll tell you later," Roberta said to allay her concern. "Both of us need a plate of food."

"How about you?" the woman asked, turning to Slocum.

"This is Slocum, Gloria."

"Nice to meet you. What'll you have?"

"The same as her."

"Take me a minute—"

"We're fine," Roberta said, and looked for his nod of approval. "Meanwhile, I can pour our coffee."

Gloria swept her prematurely gray hair back from her face. "I'd appreciate that."

She left. Gloria was an ample-bodied woman, but there wasn't much fat on her. The strain of her situation showed in the small lines around her mouth and eyes. The lack of help and maybe something else were putting a strain on her.

Roberta got up to get them some coffee, and on her way back she refilled cups at the other tables while making friendly conversation. Most folks apologized for her brother's fate. Slocum could hear their concern and politeness toward her.

When the man came in the café, she froze and glared at him.

Slocum turned and looked at a stranger in his forties wearing a tailored brown suit. He wore a clean Boss of the Plains Stetson with a silk-rimmed brim. He put it and his walking cane on wall pegs. Then he turned and pasted on a smile for her.

"Well, how are you, Miss Roberta? Doing well, I suppose." He looked around as if expecting someone to show him to his seat.

"Gloria's in the back. She's shorthanded," Roberta said, and resumed pouring coffee.

"Ah, so you are the waitress?"

"No, Worthington," she said. "I'm helping. Here, you ain't doing anything. Pour some coffee yourself." She set the pot down on a table and turned on her heel.

"Why, Roberta, what has you so upset?"

She swept the riding skirt under her and pulled the chair up. Her good eye narrowed as hard as it had a short while before when she'd brought up the rifle on Phelps. "I ain't giving you any satisfaction, Worthington."

"Just think, in three years your brother will be a free man again."

Slocum started to get up. Rage boiled in his chest, but her hand on his forearm stopped him. "He ain't worth it," she said.

"Worth what?" the man asked, advancing a few steps toward them. "Oh, you think I'm not worth sending a proven horse thief off to prison?"

"He's fixing to have company," Slocum said.

"Oh, who would that be?"

"Two men that work for you." He wanted to use the slight pause to set Worthington up. "Dawson and Manley. They do work for you, don't they?"

"What are you talking about?"

"They're in the county jail down the street." Slocum hooked a thumb in the direction of the jail. "Maybe you need to go bail them out. They said you'd hired them to work over brands and they're ready to testify in court to that. You'll still have time to catch some of the hot weather down there at Yuma."

"Mister—I don't know who you are, but when did you get to be the damn law around here?"

Slocum rose to straddle the chair. "My name's Slocum and when the special judge arrives, maybe a grand jury can indict you as an accomplice to their artwork."

"Mister, you—" Red-faced, he shook his finger at Slocum. "You are going to rue the day you threatened me. I mean it."

"That suit won't look near as nice covered in rock dust down there along the Colorado."

"Who gave you the authority anyway to arrest anyone?"

"Mister, it's part of the federal law. A citizen can arrest lawbreakers—especially self-confessed lawbreakers."

"If you aren't out of this county in twenty-four hours, have your coffin ready."

"Is that a threat?"

"No, it's a promise." Worthington started for the door, then remembered his hat and cane.

"Worthington?"

"I'm not talking—"

"You better listen to me. There are over a dozen people in here just overheard you threaten my life. If I'm dead or alive, they can tell the grand jury exactly what you said."

"There'll be no fucking grand juries in this county." He spat out the words like a venomous snake; in his departure, he slammed the door.

A cheer went up around the café. Gloria tossed a lock of hair back as she came out of the kitchen with their plates of food. "What did you do to His Majesty?"

"Ran him off," a toothless customer at the bar shouted and slapped his thighs. "Did the best damn job I ever seed of it. You missed it all, Glory. You missed it all. Why, he tied a tin can on that bastard's tail and sent him kiting."

"Amen," another yelled.

"I could hear most of it," said Gloria. "You a lawyer, too?" she asked Slocum.

"No, ma'am."

"Well, you sure sounded like one. I'll get you two some bread in a minute. It's about done in the oven." She nodded to a man putting money down near her register. "Thanks, Howard. You need change?"

The man shook his head and smiled. "Bob, you've got yourself a real one there."

"Thanks, Dub. Maybe we'll all see some daylight around here one of these days."

"I hope so." Then he shook his head as if that might not be possible and left.

Slocum looked at his heaping plate of sliced roast beef, potatoes, and gravy with brown beans, and smiled. It all looked good. He met Bob's gaze.

She closed her good eye and shook her head. "Well, you've done it all now. Joined me, arrested two of his men, and made Charles Worthington mad as a wet hen, plus made Phelps angry. I can't think of a thing you left out."

Busy cutting his meat, he nodded. "I like to get to the bottom of things fast."

She chuckled. "You damn sure did."

He wasn't even close to it, though—he wanted the wheels of justice to creak into action. That might require a fast ride to Prescott to see the governor himself. A territorial sheriff had few constraints besides the court system, and the governor could make some adjustments in that.

Despite Slocum's protests, Roberta paid for supper, and after a few kind words from Gloria, they were out in the night on the boardwalk.

"I can drive those horses home," he offered.

"I accept."

"You're easy enough to convince," he said, helping her up into the rig.

She looked back and shook her head. "I'd've made it, but thanks. I can't recall anyone ever helping me into a rig."

"Maybe they never figured you needed any help," he said, and went to tie Baldy to the tailgate.

When he came back and climbed up beside her, he took the reins. "It don't hurt to be a woman once in a while."

"No, I guess it doesn't. I'll have to learn how."

"That's not a bad idea." He set the team in jig trot under the spray of a thousand stars. It would be late when they reached the ranch. It had been a long day since he'd set his saddle down on the hillside above her place. He still had to recover his bedroll, but sharing the seat with her wasn't half bad. Not half bad at all.

In the pearl light of a quarter moon and ten million stars, they were both dog tired as they unhitched the team by the unmoving windmill.

"I don't have a bunkhouse." She rose and looked over at him. "My brother and I grew up together in that house. You can sleep in his bed. I personally don't give a damn about what's proper and what ain't, especially after last night."

"I'll respect your boundaries."

She moved to the front and unhooked the tongue from the collar on one of the horses. "I never doubted that."

He did the same to the other horse, and then he set down the tongue pole.

"No wife, no family?" she asked before starting for the gate.

"Never had a wife. My brother was killed in the war.

The rest are dead or in ashes. I'll get the harness off and toss it on the fence."

"I guess I'll do it. I've done this for years."

"That was before you hired me."

She laughed and backed up to the corral to rest her butt against it. "First day's work's going to be twenty-four hours long."

"I've had worse days." He led the horses over to the corral and she opened the gate.

"You know, we've stepped on some toes tonight." She closed the gate with him out and the team loose inside.

"Maybe they should have been stomped on a long time ago." He looked at the outline of the house in the silver light. He needed to keep to his place, though after the ride back together on the buggy seat, he felt like reaching out and hugging her shoulder. Better for now to keep his hands to himself.

He ambled along beside her to the dark porch and opened the door. Every muscle in his body ached and his mind felt cobwebbed. She lit a lamp and pointed to the far bed. "That's yours."

"Thanks. Good night."

"Good night." And she blew out the lamp.

Undressed and in the bed under the flannel sheet, he thought about the night before—all that walking. Here he had a real bed. And an attractive woman for a boss. Where did he know that Phelps from? That deputy's face had niggled him the whole way home. But nothing came. Phelps wasn't his name the last time they'd met. It would come to him . . .

Chapter 3

He awoke to discover the front door was open and light was streaming in the room. He slipped off the bed and pulled on his pants. His eyes were gritty and his mouth felt like·a barefoot army had marched back and forth through it all night. Crossing the room barefooted to the bucket on the dry sink, he dipped out a gourd of water. He was halfway through drinking it when Roberta came in with an armload of split stove wood.

She looked amazingly fresh, much better-spirited than the day before, and her smile was contagious. "I see you're up?"

"Do you have a cow to milk or pigs to slop?"

"No."

"Good. I'll grease the mill this morning, then try to re-cover my bedroll."

"Sit down. We'll have breakfast and then we better go find your bedroll. You sure you remember where you left it?"

"I think so." He put the gourd back, then went for his boots and shirt.

She stoked the fire that had started in the range, and stood up. "Biscuits, ham, and fried potatoes sound like it'll fill you?"

He started to pull on his second boot. "I'm fine with anything you want to cook."

Dressed, he started for the door. "I can saddle the horses and have them ready when we finish."

"Sure. It'll take a little time to get it all cooked."

"Besides, my bedroll ain't going to hatch or sprout anything."

She laughed and he went out. In the corral, he roped Baldy, who stopped dead when the rope went over his ears. Talking softly to him, Slocum walked up the rope. When Baldy was tied, he went after Shoo Fly, a dark horse that Roberta said she rode a lot. The gelding acted foxy, but Slocum made an overhead toss and caught him the first time. Shoo Fly bucked and kicked in a circle as Slocum reeled him in. He acted walleyed and snorted, but settled some when Slocum got to his head and formed a halter. Soon, he was tied beside Baldy. Slocum retuned with his own saddle and pads, plus a comb and brush.

He cleaned off Baldy's back and brushed him down, even cleaned the dirt off his legs and fetlock. Then he thinned Baldy's tail some before he put on the pads and saddle. Shoo Fly shifted back and forth; Slocum soon had enough of him and slapped him with the brush. The action settled him some, but in no time, he was back to whining and raising Cain. Finished with him, Slocum went to the barn for Roberta's rig.

She rang the school bell as he finished cinching Shoo Fly up. When he led the horses up to the hitch rack, she came to the door. "You do good work."

He smiled and tied the reins. "Part of the job."

"Well, you better come wash up and eat. That's part of it, too."

He looked around for anything out of place and saw nothing wrong. "Coming."

The meal was tasty and the potatoes crisply fried. He savored the coffee and dreaded hitting the saddle as he sipped on his last cup. Meanwhile, she was putting on some shotgun chaps and then her spurs. When she was finished, she stomped her heels on the wood floor.

"I'll miss old Ring. He was a guard and pal."

He rose. "I'm sorry I ain't had time to bury him."

"I didn't mean that—I—I'll just miss him."

She dropped her chin and pursed her lips. "Those sonsabitches—that damn Phelps. You saw that banty rooster yesterday."

"He always been in this country?"

"Why?"

"I think I've seen him somewhere else, but his name wasn't Phelps there."

"Ain't no telling. He drifted in here about three years ago. I think from Texas. Damn banty rooster is what he reminds me of. Strutting around like he was some kind of a ladies' man."

Her look turned dark. It was filled with hatred, and he didn't blame her. He realized that she had came close to settling it all in the sheriff's office the night before with her rifle. Only his efforts had kept her from doing it—which had saved Phelps. Not that he felt Phelps hadn't earned it—but the aftermath would have been hard on her. They'd have tried to prove it was cold-blooded murder, and she might not have told them about the night when he stole her innocence.

As they crossed the country on their quest, they looked some of the cattle over, and he spotted three more cattle with AX brands in the brush.

"What can I do about that?" she asked.

"Who's the brand inspector?"

"What can he do?"

"He can make note of the problem and straighten it out."

She shook her head. "He's not going to buck Worthington or the courthouse bunch."

"It's his job. Is the inspector in with the sheriff?"

"Gantry does whatever Worthington tells him. And he's the chief law officer in the county."

"I think brand inspectors have some separation from local law."

"His name's Billy Hayes. But I'm telling you, it ain't going to do any good. I'd bet those rustlers are back using a running iron by this morning."

Slocum shook his head. There had to be a way to stop them and he was going to find it. He remembered that pompous Worthington in the café. He looked like a bloated cow that needed deflating.

"I want to swing by the tules. I need to check that area often," she said. "Stock gets out in them and gets bogged."

"Sure," he said, taking note of the hills and where he thought he'd left his bedroll. She turned off and they rode east. In a short while, they reined up and looked over a large patch of marsh with cattails that the Spanish called tules. He drew out his telescope and scoped the area, which was alive with many birds. He saw nothing, but in places the reeds were shoulder high and might conceal an animal caught in the mud.

"I'll ride around this way, you go that way, and we can meet on the other side," she said.

He agreed, and turned Baldy north. He was about a quarter of the way around the marsh, being scolded by some red-winged blackbirds, when she gave a shout. He rode Baldy up high enough to see her waving her hat, and headed in her direction. She must have found a bogged animal. With Baldy in a long trot, he rode that way around the marsh. Hauling cattle out of mud was never an easy deal, and once out, they'd even fight you like you'd been the cause of their previous predicament. Roberta was sitting her horse, studying the longhorn steer with over half of his belly in the mud while he was shaking his horns and tossing his head.

Oh, he'd be a sweet one to recover.

"He's in pretty deep," she said, rocking on her saddle horn.

"There's lot of pear cactus down here, too." He made a sweep with his hands to indicate the numerous prickly pear beds that were on the slopes they'd need ride between to haul him out of the mud. "Just watch them."

He undid the rope and shook loose a loop. With three twirls above his head, he tossed the loop over the grunting critter's horns and jerked the slack, so the rope was around their base.

The steer began to bawl and really fight when he discovered he was caught. Slocum handed her the rope.

"Dally that around your horn and start between those two beds. Don't let him pull you or that pony down and into the cactus. We'll be all day getting the thorns out of you."

She nodded under her straw hat, but he thought he might have embarrassed her with his comment. Quickly, she wrapped the rope around the horn and spurred the bay horse to take up the slack. When the rope was tight across her right leg, the stout pony dug in and the steer began to really bawl. He thrashed, but was still stuck and facing inside rather than out. Slocum wanted him turned around so they could pull him out headfirst and use some of the steer's power to get him on the bank. This way, the steer was not able to help them—like it or not.

With the steer bawling his lungs out and the pony scratching gravel and putting his belly to the ground, they tried to turn the big critter some. On foot, Slocum worked the lariat, hoping that by pushing when the rope was taut, he might make the difference and get the steer turned around.

"We're doing it. We're doing it," she said through clenched teeth.

"Yes, yes," he agreed. The big steer was twisted some. "Rest your horse a little."

She let up on the slack and he went for Baldy. He rode back and dallied the rope on the horn. Guiding the pony between the patch of pear where there was some space, he realized that he didn't dare go much past it for the slope was too steep there for a horse to pull well. Damned if did and damned if he didn't.

He winked at her. "He's really stuck."

"And he'll come out mad as a wet hen."

Slocum nodded, and booted Baldy to haul the steer out. The pony responded and his shoes clattered on the gravel as he dug in. Slocum looked back and watched the steer's rubber neck being pulled sideways. Baldy was digging in and grunting with all his might. The rope across Slocum's leg was digging in, and he felt a little give and could see the steer was coming up.

"Get ready to clear out," he shouted to Roberta, and put his heels to Baldy. Looking back, he could see the critter's front hooves were seeking new mud and his brown belly mark was above the surface. Baldy was making good progress.

With every inch his pony gained, the more Slocum realized the steer was coming out. It was slow, but he was positive the steer would soon be on dry land. At last the bovine, screaming in madness, had his front hooves on solid ground. Slocum tossed the lariat aside and sent Baldy cat-hopping up the slope to escape the steer.

Roberta and her bay were climbing the hill fifty feet away, and they stopped short of the top to look back at the angry bovine pitching its horns. Standing feet apart like a half-dipped piece of candy, he made a wild sight.

"He sure doesn't appreciate us saving him, does he?" she asked with a grin.

"Ungrateful devil, I'd say."

"I'm just glad we didn't have to go in there and help him more."

Slocum laughed. "I was thinking the same thing."

"Searle and I have done that."

"So have I." Slocum shook his head and they rode north. "Cost you a rope 'cause I ain't going after it."

She looked back at the protesting steer and laughed. "I'm not either. I've got more at the house."

When they were near the place where he'd left his bedroll, he spotted a mottled-faced cow with her nose full of pear pads.

"How did she get into them?" Roberta looked disgusted.

"Probably grazing too close and tossed her head at a fly and caught them."

"How we going to catch her? We only have one rope."

"Run her up in the canyon and I'll heel her. Give me your lariat."

"That won't be easy in that brush."

"Ain't been nothing easy since I came here." He removed his felt hat and wiped his wet forehead on his sleeve. With the rope in his hand, they set in after the cow in a jog trot. She looked gaunt. Obviously, the bristled pads had interfered with her grazing.

The mesquite was thicker in the canyon, and they were soon forced to ride single file. They came to a clearing and he swung the rope, booted Baldy in hard to catch the cow, and slung the loop around her legs. He raised the rope and when he saw her step in the loop, he dallied it around the saddle horn and set Baldy down.

Roberta shouted, "You got her." And bailed off her horse.

"Get two sticks to pull the pads off," he shouted. "Don't use your hands."

"I won't." She searched around, found some sticks, and raced for the bawling cow on the ground. It required two tries to get the pads off with her sticks, and the head-tossing cow was no help.

At last, with the cow free of cactus, Roberta smiled in approval.

"Great," he said. "Get on your pony. I can shake the rope loose. She'll be on the prowl, too."

"Ungrateful devils." Roberta put a boot in her stirrup and swung up in the saddle, then reined the pony around.

With Roberta and her horse trotting out of the clearing, Slocum rode in and pitched enough slack that the loop came loose. Since cattle got up hind feet first, Slocum turned Baldy and rode hard after Roberta. The old heifer showed her athletic skills and soon was on the prod on Baldy's heels, trying to hook him with a horn. Slocum leaned forward and gave the pony his head. Baldy shot out and quickly left the mad cow to shake her horns at them in the distance.

Slocum coiled up the lariat and winked at Roberta. "Damn ungrateful livestock you own."

"They sure are." She rode in looking impressed, and clapped him on the arm. "Don't let anyone tell you that you ain't a cowboy. You damn sure are a good one."

He acknowledged her compliment with a smile. "We better get that bedroll."

"Shoot, I'd about forgot what we came for."

"We've sure been distracted."

An hour later, he found the bedroll where he'd left it in the mesquite tree, and they ate some biscuits filled with ham that she'd fixed for their lunch. They sat in the shade, as they ate. He held up his sandwich. "This is damn good, too."

She shrugged off his compliment. "I can cook some, but it isn't my calling."

"Got me fooled."

"Slocum, I need to hold this ranch together for the next three years. Somehow, some way, till Searle gets back and can help me."

"That might be a tall order."

"Would you stay that long?"

"Can't." He shook his head ruefully. "There's two deputies out of Fort Scott, Kansas, riding my tail. Sooner or later, word will get out I'm up here. A drunk in a bar will spout off or some teamster will get a little tipsy and say, 'I seen old Slocum in Tucson,' and they'd be down here in a few days."

"What happened?"

"A kid, maybe eighteen, lost some money at cards, got drunk, came back packing a gun, and demanded his money back. I tried to talk him out of it." Slocum shook his head. "He drew. I had no choice."

"That's self-defense."

"Not when your grandfather owns the bank, the town, and the judge. He even foots the bill for those two deputies."

"I guess you have enough problems of your own without mine."

"Hey, I'll help you as long as I can."

She reached over, clasped his forearm, and looked him in the eye. "For however long that is, I'll be pleased."

"We may get it all cleared up before I have to leave here."

He rose and she did the same. They were only a foot apart. Her good eye looked like a liquid pool of chocolate and the smudge of dust on her cheek like a blemish. He reached out and brushed the dust away with the back of his forefinger.

"Just some dust," he said.

"Oh, I must look so nice."

"You do. You're a beautiful woman."

A red flush came to her cheeks. "Yeah, but damaged."

Slowly, he shook his head and reached out to cradle her face between his calloused hands. "No one could ruin you. Not Phelps. Not the worthless deputies. They hurt you, but they never ruined you—"

His mouth touched hers, and it must have shocked her for a moment; then she threw her arms around his neck and pressed her lips to his. It knocked his hat off, but he didn't care and wasn't going to let it upset him. There would be plenty of time later to recover his weather-beaten hat—better things were in his arms. Her firm breasts felt buried in his chest. He held her hard to him as his mind spun around like a boy's top.

Her mouth opened and his tongue tested her teeth, like feeding on honeycomb. He savored the closeness of her willowy body to his own. He stopped, and let her catch her breath.

"You all right?" he asked.

"Is that why you stopped?" Out of breath, she looked up at him bleary-eyed.

"I don't want to take advantage of you."

She pulled his face back to hers for more. "I'll be the judge of that."

"Hmmm," was all he managed before their mouths meshed.

He finally swept her up and carried her to where the dark pony was grazing through the bits. "You better get on your horse."

He shifted her in his arms as he walked toward the horse.

"You afraid of me?"

"No." He set her on her feet and looked down into her face. "I'm afraid of myself."

"I'm not."

He shook his head and wiped his bare forehead on his sleeve. "I am."

"I guess we can settle this later?"

He nodded, kissed her quickly, then went for his hat and Baldy.

With the bedroll tied on behind his saddle, they started for home. They were back by late afternoon. As they descended the hillside, Slocum spotted a horse tied at the hitch rack.

"We've got company."

She nodded, squinting to try and make the animal out. "I don't know who that horse belongs to."

He shifted the Colt out of habit. Friend or foe, they'd soon learn all about it. When they reached the hard-packed open ground in front of the house and corrals—she brightened.

"It's my neighbor, Caleb Anderson."

"Good," Slocum said, relieved it wasn't someone connected with Phelps and the sheriff. They'd come around soon enough.

"What brings you out, Caleb?" she asked, dismounting, and the gray-headed man behind the bushy mustache waded over in his bull-hide chaps and gave her a fatherly hug. "Oh, that's Slocum. Meet Caleb, my neighbor. He owns the Cross P."

Slocum extended his hand to the short, thin, older cowman.

"Nice to meet you," said Caleb. "Roberta's my girl. I come over to check on her. Them no-accounts in Antelope Springs sent the wrong man to prison."

"I understand that."

"Well, you two stirred up things in town bringing in those Worthington hands."

"They still in jail?" she asked.

"No, they're out on bond. They'll flee the county. Won't be any trial. But you knew that."

"I figured something like that would happen. Who bailed them out?" Slocum asked.

"I don't know for certain, but my guess would be Worthington did. He couldn't afford them going on trial and talking."

Slocum agreed.

"I'll fix supper for us," Roberta said. "Won't be much, but you two can talk and put up the horses." She excused herself and headed for the house.

Slocum led the ponies, and Caleb ambled along with him in the fashion of most older men who'd been broken up in a hundred horse wrecks.

"How's she doing?" Caleb glanced back to be sure she wasn't in hearing.

"She'd've done a damn sight better if them three hadn't been waiting for her and jumped her when she got back from seeing Searle taken off."

Caleb caught his arm. "Who done that?"

"Phelps and two other deputies, she said."

His blue eyes narrowed to a hawk's hard look. "You telling me they raped her?"

Slocum stopped at the tank to let the horses drink. He began undoing the latigos. "That's what she told me."

Caleb threw his weather-beaten felt hat in the dust and stomped his boot. "Why, them no-account worthless sons a bitches."

"I thought the same thing, but we've got to be careful. It would be her word against theirs. Three to one. She's got too much pride to go on the stand and go through a trial."

"I had no idea," Caleb said, and swept up his hat. "That makes me so damn mad I could spit nails. Where did they get the damn nerve?"

"They're behind that badge."

He twisted his mustache ends and his red face looked like he was ready to boil.

Slocum glanced at the house, and then removed his saddle from Baldy. "Better act like you don't know anything about it."

Caleb agreed. "I will. I will, but my lands, she was hurt bad enough by them sending Searle to jail on them made-up charges. Heavens, he's just a boy. Tough boy, but man, Yuma prison is a hellhole."

"That has her upset, too."

"I bet. Why I came over was to check on her. You just happen along?"

"My horse colicked the night before and I came in on foot that morning right after them three left. I saw their fresh tracks in the road. They shot her stock dog, too."

"Them worthless devils. When I rode in, I wondered where he was at." Caleb shook his head as he carried her saddle and pads to the shed with Slocum. "What can we do?"

"I'm not certain. See how things pan out. Then maybe we can figure out a way to pay all these bastards back."

"Count me in—any way I can help."

"Good."

"You hanging around?"

"For a while."

"That's good. Obvious that she needs some protection here," Caleb said, putting her saddle on the rack.

When the horses were in the lot and rolling in the dust, Slocum and Caleb went to the house and washed up.

From the porch, Slocum looked off to the west where the low sun was bleeding in the sky. Doves cooed and quail scurried out in the dry grass and chaparral. The windmill creaked, powered by the late afternoon wind—it needed greasing. Cottonwood leaves rattled. Heavenly place for all the hell that had taken place there of late.

She called them to supper.

Chapter 4

Dawn found Slocum looking over the shallow tank and dam with the connecting ditch that irrigated the ten to twelve acres of barley stubble when there was enough water. Now, in the summer, the water was low, and he could see it would require a substantial runoff to fill up again, but whoever had built the system knew a lot about irrigation.

The night before, Caleb had stayed until midnight playing rummy before he rode off for his own place. After their company left, they both were too tired to do anything but kiss, fall in their own beds, and sleep. He'd woken when a rooster quail got to bragging out in the chaparral in the predawn. The still house was dark when he'd dressed and started his survey of the place.

The irrigation project grew enough forage for their horses.

"Dad wanted to grow alfalfa," she said, wrapped in a robe and standing on the rise behind him.

"Not enough water?"

"Not enough, but he dreamed about it."

"Are there any artesian wells in this country?"

"I don't know of any. Most wells are like the one at the windmill, hand-dug. Besides, I couldn't afford a driller."

"Are there any drills in the country?"

She shrugged and smoothed the robe wrapped tight around her willowy figure. "It would simply cost too much."

"Ever hear of miracles?"

"No. Not in my life." She shook her head. "They don't happen."

He climbed up the grade and shielded his eyes with his hand from the piercing glare. "There must be sixty or more acres here that could be irrigated in this flat if you had the water."

She nodded. "Dad thought so when he homesteaded this section. But the tank's never been full enough to do more than the patch we cleared. Some years, we're lucky to even water half of it."

"I can see that." Unable to hold back any longer, he swept her up in his arms and started for the house with his precious cargo.

She looked embarrassed. "I didn't come up here to—to—lure you."

"Hey. I'm glad you came. I couldn't help myself."

She pulled his face down to hers and he stopped to kiss her. Honey flowed from her mouth and he grew heady, striding across the rise.

She gulped for her breath. "Not—not on my bed."

"Whatever you say."

"I want no reminders of that night."

He nodded, and hurried a little faster going down the slope for the house. Once over the threshold and into the house's shady, cool interior, he set her down and kissed her. Then he closed the door and barred it.

She led him by a finger to his bed and fumbled with his shirt buttons. When his shirt was undone and open, she rested her cool forehead on his chest. "I'm scared."

"I don't blame you. We'll let it happen. You get too scared—we'll quit."

She sighed, and he lifted her chin. Then his mouth

closed on hers and he squeezed her tight to him. Slowly, a fire began to rise in her. A hungry flame in need of more fuel. Her palms squeezed his face and her mouth became a volcano. She forced his shirt off while he toed off his boots. He untied the ropelike belt of the robe, and slid his hand in to cup her firm pear-shaped breast. As he used his thumb in a circular fashion, the nipple rose to a hard point.

Their mouths demanding more of each other, they whirled in passion's dance. His pants fell and he stepped clear of them, pushing the robe off her shoulders so her bare skin was against his.

When she dropped on the bed, she gasped at what she saw of his erection, and then the fear in her face melted and she smiled. "Come to me."

He followed her across the bed, filled with a need to seek her depths. Sprawled on her back, she held her arms out for him. He moved in and kissed her hard.

She squirmed to be under him, and he parted her legs to get between them. His hand cupped her mound and his thumb spread open her gates. Satisfied she was moist enough for his entry, he raised her knees up and then inserted the throbbing skintight head in the lips.

Gently, he probed against the ring. She clutched his arms as if she anticipated pain. The way was tight, and he took his time to work in and out to lubricate his way. The muscles in his butt screamed for him to stab her, but he refrained, opening the way more and more each time with gentle pushes against it. Then he eased his rock-hard dick through the restriction and she gasped with a sigh, "Oh, yes."

He smiled down at her. Her face was half hidden by her hair and by the shadowy light in the room. Her fingers slipped off his arms and she fell into never-never land under him.

In a short while, his actions began to quicken. She

wrapped her legs around him and hunched to meet his thrusts. Her mouth open, she moaned in pleasure's arms and tossed her head. Then, seized by it all, she began to rock on her back faster and faster until she cried out with a hard strain. A hot rush of fluid surrounded his dick and he smiled.

Then she fainted. Parting the hair over her face, she blinked at him and gasped, "What was that?"

"You having fun."

"Oh, my God. I don't even know where I am."

"You'll be all right. Hang on."

She did, and in a short while he had her back in a whirlwind vortex. Both of them soon strained and the sparks flew, until he came and they both collapsed in a pile side by side.

"Oh, my God, Slocum." She threw her arm over him and squeezed his body to her. "I was raped by boys."

"Boys?"

"They had—well, they were smaller than a dog. Yodder never could get it hard enough to go in me." She buried her face in his chest. "I'm sorry, I shouldn't have said that. Oh, I wish it had been you first."

"It was me." He kissed her forehead.

"Yes, it was you. You were first."

She began to kiss the fine hair on his chest, and when he moved against her, she sucked in her breath. "You aren't finished, are you?"

"It's your call."

She rolled on her back. "Don't wait for me. I'm ready."

Later, he went to the hillside and buried the dog's remains, while she cleaned up and fixed breakfast. He had the grave completed when she called to him.

"I'll be there shortly." Using the shovel, he put the corpse in the grave and then covered it. Shovel on his shoulder, he headed back for the house, grateful that the job was completed.

Then, he heard the hard-running horses and the sound of a buckboard coming off the hill. In the distance, a fan of dust trailed it.

"Who's coming?" she asked, standing in the doorway and wearing an apron over her riding garb.

"Don't know. But he's in a hurry, that's for sure."

The driver swung the team around and as the veil of dust cleared, a stern-faced man in a suit covered with dust reared back on the reins as he sat on the spring seat.

"What brings the sheriff out here today?" she asked the man.

"Who's he?" The man indicated Slocum.

"My foreman."

"Slocum's my name. I never caught yours." He never offered to shake the man's hand.

"Hmm." The man set a scowl on his face. "Why didn't you report the rustling?" he asked Roberta.

"I did. I brought both them brand changers to your jail and filed the warrant."

"You have a witness?"

"Slocum here."

"They say they're innocent."

Her eyelashes narrowed at him. "You lose the confession they signed?"

"Ah, ah, no. But it's your word against theirs."

"Gantry, we brought them to you, with a signed confession from each of them, and we can get the steer they marked up. Now what more do you want?"

"Court cases cost the county lots of money that we don't have."

"Never was a problem when you trumped up them charges against Searle."

"And what's this threat about a special judge? What are you up to?"

"I figure a judge that don't get paid off by Charles

Worthington might run an honest court, and the governor might just send one."

"You don't have no proof of that."

"You'd be surprised what all I do know."

"Well—it—won't do you no good."

"Them two rustlers worked for Worthington. When that pair tells a grand jury that they were under his orders to mark them brands like that, then maybe there's a bunk in Yuma Prison for him, too."

Gantry's face grew red. "There won't be no grand jury in this county."

"Maybe. Maybe not, but you can squirm awhile on that one. A governor has lots of authority in a territory when push comes to shove."

"I'm warning you. You push this thing too far and your brother might never get out of that hellhole alive."

Slocum caught her arm and frowned her down. When he was satisfied that she was in control of herself, he turned back to Gantry.

"You've made some big threats here this morning. For a man of the law, you've stepped on both sides of it. I understand as tax collector you make a healthy sum. I'd be more worried about losing that honey hive than I would about losing Worthington. Ranchers ever learn you're in cahoots with a rustler, they'll turn you out of office quicker than a lamb can swish its tail."

"Mister—I'm the law here."

"Don't give me that crap. Ask them three deputies of yours where they were the afternoon they shipped her brother out."

She gave a gasp behind him.

"Go ahead. Get the truth out of them."

"What about them?"

"You're the law. You ask them what they did that afternoon and evening."

Gantry shook his finger at Slocum. "You better listen to me, saddle tramp!"

"No, you're the one needs to listen. But I fear it's too late to save your hide."

"We'll see who runs the law in this county." He slapped the heated horses and whirled away.

Roberta rushed over and hugged Slocum. "Why did you tell him that?"

"He'll pressure them boys till they tell him. Then that'll worry him some more. He didn't know a thing about it. I could see I blindsided him with it."

With her eyes wet, she looked up at him. "I won't testify."

"I didn't expect you to. I only wanted another porcupine quill stuck in him."

"Can he hurt Searle in prison?"

"Naw, that was just a threat." But he wasn't convinced about what he said—enough money could do anything.

Slocum watched Gantry's dust go over the hill. They weren't rid of anything. Least of all Worthington or the sheriff's department.

Chapter 5

"There's a mining village called Barlowville north of here. I think I can mail a letter to the governor from there with Gantry none the wiser."

Slocum nodded as they sat eating their cold breakfast. "You better get to writing. I'll make a swing by the marsh and look around. Be back in mid-afternoon. You keep a gun close and don't take any chances."

"You do the same. We can post it tomorrow. It's a tough ride over there, but we can make it in a few hours. Well, maybe we should take our bedrolls."

He winked at her. "Might take them for show."

She blushed and got up for more coffee. It was hot on the stove. "You know, I never thought about that—looking respectable."

"Request that the chief brand inspector comes out and surveys the damage done here, too," he told her.

"What good will that do?"

"A brand inspector requested to check things out would have to reply to the governor about his findings. That might get more action out of the courts."

"You're probably right."

He finished his fresh coffee, kissed her good-bye, and

went after Baldy. When he rode by the house, she ran out with some food wrapped in a cloth.

"So you don't starve."

He threw her another kiss, saluted her, and rode on. Seemed a shame to go off and leave her all alone, but he had things he wanted to see again. Check more of her cattle for blotched brands, see about the bogs, and learn the lay of the land. A good knowledge of the country could pay big dividends any time he needed to know something.

At mid-morning, he rode up a side canyon to check it out. Five javelinas ran out of the juniper and live oak brush headed for new ground. Baldy spooked to the side. Slocum checked him, and laughed when he realized that the piglike critters were as surprised as he and the pony were. The narrow trail wound upward until he reached a spring flow that crossed the trail. The water had attracted the javelinas.

There was a brush lean-to nearby and other signs that someone had camped there. But the signs and tracks he saw were not recent enough for him to care who had made them. Could be renegade Indians—there were still several of them on the loose in Arizona and Sonora. Loners, for the most part. Dangerous, too.

His hat in hand, he studied the towering walls of brown and tan layers. There was nothing in the azure sky but a buzzard riding on the updrafts. The narrow chasm led to the top, so after Baldy had a drink, Slocum remounted and rode him to the pass.

Wind swept his face, and he could see lots more broken country spread beneath him. He rested Baldy for a few minutes, then mounted up and started back down.

Who had used the camp? Prospector or renegade? He rode on by the water source, and the clack of Baldy's shoes on the rocks rang like a bell and then echoed back. Out in the open country dotted with junipers, he set Baldy in a trot for the home place, spooking up a set of cows and calves. Mostly brockle-faced, longhorn-Hereford cows sporting three-quarter calves that showed good. Even a loafing horned white-face bull rose out of the shade, stretched his back, and then moved off with the cows and calves.

Her outfit impressed him. She had a good cow outfit going. If she could hold it together till her brother got out of prison, she might someday have an empire, or at least a damn good ranch.

At mid-afternoon, he rode in and dismounted at the hitch rack. He'd found nothing out of place. No cattle in the bog. He looked up when she appeared in the door in a robe. Her hair was wet and she was busy drying it. "Didn't expect you back so soon."

He turned on his heel and went back to Baldy like he was leaving.

"No, I mean, I didn't expect you back so soon. Don't leave."

He laughed, and caught her in his arms and hugged her. "Seen lots of country. You know that trail goes over the hills back there?"

"Dead Man's Spring?"

"I guess. How did it get that name?"

"Some prospector was killed up there years ago by Apaches. The war party found two baking powder cans full of gold nuggets in his things that the Apaches scattered all over."

"Anyone find the mine?"

"No, and not much gold in the creek beds to indicate there is any in those hills."

He followed her inside. "Where did the gold come from?"

She shrugged and began brushing her hair. "Some think he may have high-graded it up at the Vulture Mine. You know, stole it while working up there. It was the same kind as that ore. The gold came from a white-quartz source, and there isn't much white quartz up there."

"Guess we'll never know, huh?"

She stopped brushing her hair and smiled at him. "I could sure use that gold if I ever found it."

"Who couldn't use it? You get the letter written?"

"Yes. I hope the governor reads it."

"Good, we'll ride over in the morning and mail it. Take most of the day?" He poured himself some coffee.

"Oh, yes, we can ride over. That's old stale cofffee, I—"

"It'll be just fine," he said, looking in the tin cup. "I ain't use to babying."

"I wouldn't call it that." Pulling out a tangle with her hairbrush, she made a pained face. "I'd like to spoil you."

"You're doing that, girl."

His lower back complained in the predawn light. He stopped saddling a bay gelding Roberta called Cy, and put his hands on his hips to strain against the soreness. Images of her subtle body in the bed with him all night made him close his eyes. Must have awakened a devil inside that girl. He laced the latigos and drew the cinch up—he'd ride Cy today and give Baldy a day off.

Her sorrel King was saddled and, leading them both, he strode back to the house in the cool air. The chaparral was waking up. Wrens, doves, and quail all heralded the coming new day. At the hitch rack, he tied on the bedrolls she'd set out earlier.

"You must know how long it takes me to cook," she said from the doorway, and swept back an errant wave of hair from her face.

"When I smelled it, I went to working faster." He washed his hands at the basin set out, and dried them on the floursack towel on the nail.

She hugged his arm and herded him inside. "It is so peaceful here with you. I hate to leave."

He agreed, and hung his hat on the peg.

After doing the breakfast dishes, they left the ranch and headed north for Barlowville. A big jackrabbit kicked up by their approach loped to the first rise to see who was coming. The trail and dim wagon tracks it followed led through the mesquite and when they gained elevation, they could see where junipers studded the grassland. It was a country that any cowman could appreciate. Several small bunches of cows raised up from their grazing to look the two riders over in their passing.

"Dad believed in the Hereford breed," she said. "He had some of the first in this part of the territory. Guess it got contagious from there."

"He had lots of vision."

She nodded, riding stirrup to stirrup with him. "Shame that his heart quit—he was only fifty-five."

"A real shame. He built a fine ranch. You and your brother have a good start."

"Yeah, and him in prison—maybe the governor will look into it."

"It's a good notion."

"I hope so. Look." She pointed out a mule deer and her two fawns taking to the brush.

"Plenty of game left in this country," he said.

"There's some mountain lions that come through, too. They got a colt of mine back in the early spring."

"They make big circles. Hard to catch them short of some good hounds."

"I need one of those. But worse than that, I hate losing Ring. He was sure a big help working cattle in the brush."

They were getting higher—a few scrub cedars marked the land. Large beds of prickly pear covered the ground. Some they rode by had been eaten on by the javelinas. Their mouth marks on the pads looked funny. How anything could eat those spiny pads, he had no idea.

By noon, they were at a spring-fed tank, and the adobe ruins of a jacal and corral marked the site.

"There used to be a ranch here," he said, slaking his thirst by filling his tin cup full of water.

"It's tied up in court," she said. "The family was killed by Apaches over ten years ago. The heirs are arguing with some lawyers over it in court."

"Who's paying the lawyers?"

"Worthington, I think. He's the one wants all the land he can steal or run the owners off of."

"Interesting man."

"How's that?"

"You say he owns the sheriff. And he was behind getting your brother framed. He also is trying to buy up all this country?"

"Yes, all of that and more."

"Where does he bank?"

She blinked at him. "I don't know. Maybe at the bank in Antelope Springs. Cramer family owns it."

"No, he's got deeper pockets than that. That bank's a small-town deal."

"Why would that be important?"

"If we could convince his lender that the money he's loaned Worthington is in jeopardy, he might get upset enough to stop the supply and call in his debt."

"How do we find that out?"

"Oh, there's got to be a way."

She shook her head as if amazed at him. "You must sit up nights thinking of things."

"Not lately."

"Why?"

"Someone's been keeping me from thinking."

She looked embarrassed, then reached over and gave him a shove. "I'll just let you think more. Let's lope a ways."

Barlowville sat in a valley of tall greasewood between a parallel pair of steep hills. The gray rocky ground yielded little grass or other shrubs save for the head-high creosote-smelling bush. Eroded jacales that needed plastering had small screaming children running around them, guarded in the doorways by blank-faced Spanish women who studied Slocum and Roberta as they passed. The three cantinas were in no better condition, and the only building he saw that was not made of earthen blocks was the store and post office. It sported rusty tin siding and, save for the tattered American flag flapping over it, looked like a sagging porch—on its last legs.

Even the black dogs that came out to bark at them looked underfed. Most of them would have been culled by a Sioux squaw as too thin to butcher. Slocum and Roberta reined up at the store and dismounted. Then he loosened their cinches.

"Sure ain't the picture of prosperity," he said, twisting around to look the place over.

"I don't think these mines yield much."

He nodded, and followed her inside. She bought a three-cent stamp from the whiskered man in the dusty overalls who stood behind the barred window, which was framed by the small mailboxes.

"Ah, yes, going to our beloved territorial—"

His words were cut short by the loud entrance of a drunken Indian who stomped in cussing. He was dressed in typical Apache garb: a once-white breachcloth, leggings, and a pullover shirt. Some silver pesos coins hung from his neck on a rawhide thong. He wore a red bandanna around his head, and an old greasy eagle feather hung on the right side of his head. Strapped on his waist was a holster and six-gun that he made no move to use.

"Rip! You fuck me! I give you too much gold! You fuck me!"

Slocum looked at the man behind the counter and then at the weaving Indian—probably a breed. He wore Indian rawhide boots knee-high with pointed toes.

"Gawdamn your blanket ass, Joe Black Horse, get your worthless Digger ass the hell out of here." Rip pointed at the open front door. "I gave you credit for the rest."

"Me no Digger. Me Apache." Black Horse, or whatever his name was, was beating on his chest with his fist. He wore a silver-turquoise bracelet on his wrist.

Hands on his hips, the store man faced him down, spat on the floor, wiped his hairy mouth on the back of his hand, and then pointed at the door. "You come back sober and talk to me."

"I be back." Black Horse turned and stumbled out.

"You must know him," Slocum said after he was gone.

"Aye, I do. Black Horse's a breed. Excuse me, ma'am. But his maw got hooked on that hooch and took on them soldiers at Fort Bowie. So his father, I'd bet, was some Irish buck private." Rip shook his head. "But he has a fine mine some'ers that none of them can find."

"He have a claim?" Slocum asked.

"Why, Lord, no, laddie. He's got him a mine them Spaniards found and the Apaches killed them for taking that yellow iron out. Now them Apaches are all up at San Carlos." Rip shrugged. "He may be the only one left that knows where it is at. He might have been just a kid with a war party when they got them Spaniards, and then they concealed the mine. The rest of them renegades might all be dead save for Black Horse." Rip looked like he was satisfied that that was probably what had happened.

"What kind of a source is it coming from?" Slocum asked.

"Rose quartz. I'll show you some."

Rip took a velvet bag from the open safe and poured some of the gold out on a brass plate with a clink. They were huge nuggets. Some as big as Slocum's thumbnail. He picked up a large one and examined the traces of the rock that had been attached to it. Then he showed it to Roberta and they both nodded. Dead Man's Spring. No words were necessary.

They thanked Rip, and Slocum bought a small sack of peppermint candy before they left. With each of them sucking on a piece, they tightened their girths and swung in the saddle.

"Hey, hey," a man shouted at them, coming on the run down the dirt street. "Wait, wait. I just want to talk to someone who speaks English." He was in his early thirties and wore a snap-brim felt hat, whipcord riding pants, and knee-high English boots.

Slocum checked his horse and looked at Roberta as if to ask who he might be. She shrugged and shook her head as if she didn't know the man.

"Haney Thorpe." He made a bow, obviously enthralled at the sight of her.

"Her name's Bob, mine's Slocum."

"Well, I told you mine. I am in a bit of a fix here."

Slocum held on to the cap of his saddle horn with one hand clasped over the other. "What's that?"

"I have a well-drilling rig, but it's broken down and I have no money to fix it." He turned his palms up.

"What's broken?"

"The wheels—they must have been half rotten when they sold it to me. But if you can't move it, you can't drill wells."

"How many wheels are under it?" Had they found a drilling rig? No, this was too good to be true.

"There are twelve wheels under it—see, it is so heavy it has two wheels on each side and others on extra axles."

"How heavy is it?" Slocum asked.

"It requires eight teams of oxen to pull it."

"You have the oxen?"

"Oh, yes. They're fine."

"Let's go look at his problem," Slocum said, and turned around to look at Roberta.

She agreed, and Thorpe took off to run ahead of them while talking all the time. When they rounded the bend, Slocum could see the smokestack of the steam engine. Heavens, it must be the size of a locomotive. It was a large steam engine with reels of cable. It had to weigh ten tons.

"Why did you haul it up here?"

"I was going to drill a well for the Ferguson Brothers' mine."

"Did you drill it?"

"No. Their gold vein played out and by the time I got here, they'd closed the doors and left the country."

Slocum dismounted and began to examine the busted spokes. They were old wood and brittle, but they could be replaced.

Haney was right beside him, out of breath. "What do you think?"

"They can be repaired. Some of the other parts of the wheels will need to be repaired, but mainly you need new spokes in all the wheels."

"New wheels'll cost over a thousand dollars."

Slocum shook his head. "It will take maybe two weeks to get the lumber and make new ones."

"Where? How? When? What can I do?"

Slocum saw Roberta look away about to laugh when he put his hand on Haney's shoulder. "We're going to make a sled and take this rig to her ranch. You can drill her an artesian well with it while I rebuild those wheels."

"Huh?"

"You heard me. We're making a sled and going to slide this down to her ranch, and then while I fix the wheels, you can drill her a well."

"Is it downhill to her place?"

"No. But they had sleds before they had wheels."

He blinked his blue eyes in shock. "How far away is her place?"

"It'll take us a few days to get there by the wide route we'll need to take. While you're drilling, I'll get the wheels rebuilt."

"Can you do that?"

"Yes. To move it, I'll need to find some mine timbers for runners." Slocum looked around. Where would he find some? "You just have your teams ready. Day after tomorrow, we're hauling ass out of here."

Slocum straightened. His back already ached. With his hands on his hips, he walked over to Roberta as she held the horses. "Where's the nearest sawmill?"

"Smoothers has one over in Pine Canyon."

"Can we get there by dark?"

She shook her head. So they'd lose another day.

"I want to be at his mill at sunup. Will he take credit?"

"I suppose. He and my dad were good friends."

"Fine, let's find something to eat and set out for there."

"I can feed you," Haney said.

"Lead the way." With a wave, he sent the man on and mounted up. He wasn't sure he could stand Haney for that month or so ahead.

"Where did he come from?" she asked with a frown.

"I don't really care. I want that well drilled."

She agreed, and they followed Haney. It was going to be tough, but the solution to one of her problems could be that steam engine.

Chapter 6

Abe Smoothers was a tough man to deal with. Even in the early morning at his kitchen table, he asked lots of questions about the whole thing. He'd not heard that her brother Searle had been framed and sent to jail. But his dislike of Worthington and the current sheriff finally brought him around to agreeing to help them.

"I can send a wagonload of skid lumber over there today," he finally said. "No, we better send two. You two are in a real fix. But what if he don't strike any water?"

"We aren't even thinking that," Roberta said, passing around the biscuits that Smoothers's Chinese cook had made for their breakfast.

"We can sell it off for postholes," Slocum said.

Smoothers laughed. "Make quite a fence. While you're skidding that rig to the ranch, me and the boys here at the mill can make you some spokes. I'll need the measurements, but I've got some dry ash and walnut."

Slocum put down his fork, reached across the table, shook his hand, and thanked him. "This is going to work."

"Young man, I consider myself a good judge of men. I know them that get things done and them that talk about doing 'em. I can see you're a doer, and she sure is." Smoothers smiled and his eyes crinkled in the corners. "This may be fun. I'd like to see how it all gets done."

Slocum wasn't turning down any help, but he didn't know what Smoothers thought was fun.

They left for Barlowville in two hours. Both wagons were loaded with heavy runners. Smoothers drove four mules abreast on his wagon. Dan, his right-hand man, and a helper named Zeke drove a double team of Belgiums.

They came in a trot with a jingle of harness and an urgency that excited Slocum. They brought jacks, saws, drills, chisels, hammers, and long bolts. The project had become important to Smoothers, too.

Long past dark, they were still working by candle lamps. Smoothers crawled out from under the carriage and said the sled would work.

"We have to pull it backward about a quarter mile," Smoothers said as Roberta fed them all from a bucket of beans and bacon, filling tin plates with a dipper.

"That's downhill," he added. "We can turn it down there."

Slocum agreed. "First light, we hook the oxen."

Haney, numb from the work and all that was happening, nodded. "Then what?"

"We start for the ranch when we get it headed right."

Sitting on the ground and shaking his head, Haney acted like he could hardly eat, drumming a spoon on the side of his plate. "I never believed this would happen."

"It's going to happen. Better eat up. Sunrise, we go backward to that flat and turn it around there," Slocum said while eating his supper.

When he was through eating, Slocum rose stiffly. His hands were aching. He dropped his plate and spoon in the sudsy pail manned by one of Haney's crew. Slocum went to where Roberta had put their bedrolls. He took off his hat and seated himself cross-legged on one of them.

She soon joined him and dropped down on her roll.

"I better go back and check on things tomorrow at the ranch," she said.

He agreed. "You be double careful. Phelps ain't through. Even if he admitted to Gantry what they did to you."

"I know. I know. What if Worthington gets wind of this—"

"He may know more about this country than we do. And if he thinks well drilling'll help you, he'll sure try to stop us."

She rose on her knees and kissed him—kissed him hard. Then she looked pleadingly into his eyes. "Damn, I liked it just you and me. This is a madhouse."

"Come on. We need to find us some privacy." He slapped on his hat, then gathered his bedroll under his arm, and they went down the draw.

She clung on his arm. "No shame in me, uh?"

"Two grownups can do what they want."

"I hadn't thought about that—grownups. Yes, we are."

"I thought so."

In the starlight, she looked up at him as they hurried away from the fire's glare. "Slocum, what if we don't find water?"

"Then we tried."

"You'd gone to a lot of trouble for a try."

"That's my way."

"May be why I'm so damned infatuated with you."

He found a flat area and went to the far edge in an open spot. With a flip, he unfurled the bedroll, looked around in the silver light, and felt satisfied they were alone.

He grinned down at her considering with excitement what was about to transpire, as she cautiously unbuttoned her shirt. Then he toed off his boots. He bent over and kissed her on the mouth. He lost his hat as he swept her in his arms. A need rose in both of them. Hugging her hard to him, he tasted the honey of her lips, and the tip of his tongue traced the edge of her even teeth.

His hand under her open shirt felt the firm right breast,

and the touch made his heart quicken. With great care, he fondled the firm flesh, feeling the nipple rise like a volcano's peak. On and on they kissed, until they were out of breath. Then they tore their faces apart and gulped for air, shedding clothes like their lives depended on it.

In seconds, they were scrambling to get on top of the bedroll, skin pressed to skin, with her pulling him down on top of her with her knees raised and spread open for his entrance.

"Slocum—oh!"

His erection eased through her ring of fire and she pushed her hips at him. They were locked in passion's grip. Deep in his butt was a fierce force raging to probe her fiery furnace. Her bare heels were spurring him on as she raised her hips to meet him, and he went for more and more. The blazes raged. Her walls began to contract on his throbbing head, and the thrusts grew tighter. Then her nail-like clit began to scratch the top of his rock-hard dick. He plowed into her bottom depth, and the fire rose in his testicles and he came.

She cried out through her clenched teeth and fainted. He supported his weight over her, until slowly she began to open her bleary eyes and shake her head. "Damn you."

With a grin, braced on his arms, he pushed his still-stiff rod deeper into her. "You through?"

"No."

"Good. I wasn't either."

"I may not walk again."

"Be a shame . . ."

In the dim light of predawn, Slocum could see the yoked white steers being hooked on the long chain by the two Mexican boys and Haney. After checking their sled runners, Smoothers and his men were doing some last-minute work on a runner under lamplight.

"We're all going to have to steer using the tongue."

Smoothers clapped the dirt off his hands. "It'll take all of us to hold on to it so it don't jack under and turn the rig over."

Slocum agreed.

They ate fried corn mush that the Chinaman cooked. Haney called him Lo and he was a shy little man, who stayed back and nodded if anyone looked at him. Finishing with coffee, Slocum met Benny and Carillo, Haney's drivers.

"They're worried about this sled business," Haney said.

Slocum nodded. "It'll work, but it will be slow."

Haney nodded, and then spoke in Spanish to the two men.

Smoothers joined them, and he also spoke in Spanish to the two drivers. Then the process was ready to begin.

Roberta joined Slocum with their two saddle horses. "I'm going to watch them back up," she said. "Then I'll head out and see you tomorrow night."

Slocum agreed. Smoothers had parked one wagon and Dan, his man, drove the second one. Zeke, the older one, was with Smoothers and Haney on the tongue. The word was passed that they were ready. The oxen began to take up slack on the long chain. Whips popped. And once the chain was taut, the rig began to creak and then slide, inches at first. Then the steers began to ease the huge load along, and the men on the tongue shouted, "Hurrah!"

Chosen as the scout, Slocum rode ahead. Many adults and children lined the road to observe the event. Roberta rode with him, and acknowledged the onlookers as the creaking load came slithering along behind them.

Dan and the wagon had gone ahead, and he was already unloading some timbers for the sled to slide over a washout in the road. Slocum dismounted and joined him.

"First obstacle," Slocum said to the man in his twenties.

"Yes, sir. Howdy, ma'am." He swept his pancake wool cap off for Roberta.

"Good morning." She twisted in the saddle to look back. "It's still coming."

"Oh, unless there's a grand canyon in the way, we'll make it fine," Dan said, and went back to finishing his job. "That should do it, all right?"

Slocum agreed and remounted. He and Roberta rode ahead to where they planned to turn the rig around and then hitch the oxen to the end of the tongue. When they reined up, he leaned over and kissed her. "Be very careful," she said.

"I will. You do the same."

She short-loped southward to her place on the dim road he hoped to take this steam engine and its equipment over. Was it a fool's mission? Perhaps, but if he could get it there and strike real water—she'd be set.

Finally, the rig was turned around and rehitched. They headed south, skirting a small range of blue granite hills. The crunch of gravel under the runners and the straining sounds as the load swayed with each tilt followed them. Smoothers's cook came in a small wagon pulled by short mules. Smoothers and Dan drove ahead to look for washouts they could fill.

Slocum rode alongside them, pointing out the road's path.

"Pretty good country," Smoothers said, indicating the open land ahead. "For this job."

They took a noon break and ate some jerky that Smoothers passed out.

"I sure want to thank you for your help," Slocum said as the two squatted in some shade.

"I liked her old man. He helped me temper my first saw blade and showed me how to sharpen it better. He was smart. So I'm paying him back, plus that damn courthouse bunch ain't my favorite. They act like they own this country."

"What do you know about Worthington?"

"Acts like he has lots of money. Owes me for some lumber he got over nine months ago. Why?"

"He's the one framed her brother along with the sheriff."

Smoothers made a scowl. "What do you reckon they're up to?"

"See this rig here?"

"Yeah, I'm helping haul it."

"If there's artesian water under this ground and this rig can find it, this country will boom. I'm thinking it's their plan, too."

Smoothers looked hard at the distant purple hills. Then he agreed.

The rig creaked along well and by mid-afternoon when they stopped, Slocum estimated they'd come eight or so miles. A third of the way. Slocum dropped from the saddle and shook hands with Haney and then his two drivers, who grinned.

Slocum went to loosening his girth to unsaddle his horse and then hobble him. He'd watered him at the spring before they arrived, and he turned him loose to graze on the cured bunchgrass. With his saddle standing on the fork for the pads to dry, he spread out his bedroll. A short siesta, and then he'd ride on and check more of the road ahead.

He awoke to some loud words being exchanged. His first move was to close his fist on the redwood handles of his Colt. What was all the shouting about? Grabbing his hat, he rose and went to see about the commotion.

He saw Sheriff Gantry, with Haney and Smoothers both standing beside the sheriff's buckboard. Hot words were flying back and forth.

"What's going on with you all?" Slocum asked.

"I'm here to serve a restraining order against Haney here. He owes money to several people, and removing this drilling rig will make it impossible for them to collect."

"Who's he owe?" Slocum stepped over to the buggy.

"Right here. Landsworth Merchantile, two hundred dollars."

Slocum turned to Haney.

Haney shook his head and turned up his palms. "I never heard of them. I never signed any bills with any store."

"Who are they, Sheriff?" Slocum turned to the lawman.

"How should I know? I only serve the paper the court gives me."

Slocum nodded. "What if that is fictitious and you're only holding this man up from making a living?"

"Slocum, I just serve the papers. Park it here or I'll bring my men out and we will take custody of it until this is settled."

"Sheriff, you want to post a guard, fine, but they can just come along with us. By the way, how far away can Haney get this rig on a sled?"

"You refusing a direct order of a law enforcement officer?" Gantry's face reddened and he looked ready to pop.

"We have work to do. Now get the hell out of here. I was taking a nap."

Gantry's dark eyes narrowed and he shook the buggy whip at Slocum. "I'll—I'll see you in prison."

"You may be looking out through those bars yourself. Are those rustlers still in jail?"

"No."

"Well, when the governor gets through with you, Yuma may be your next address, or Leavenworth, Kansas."

"What in the hell are you talking about?"

"The U.S. marshal will tell you all about it."

Black with anger, Gantry shouted, "Move this rig and you will face the consequences."

Then he drove off in a cloud of dust. Good riddance. Slocum watched him and could hear him cursing the buggy horse to go faster.

Smoothers laughed. "Mentioning the governor got him all shook up."

"I'm wondering how he learned so much so quick,"

Slocum said, bewildered by the man's fast response. He had to have had a spy up at Barlowville to get word that fast that they were moving the drill rig.

Haney agreed. "Sure didn't take him long to find out."

Slocum wondered. Had they taken Roberta hostage? She wouldn't tell them much. But if they tortured her? Sumbitch—he better go check on her.

"Haney, I want to go check on Bob. If you'd load my bedroll in your wagon, that would help. I'll catch you later."

"You need any help?" Smoothers asked.

He shook his head. "Keep it rolling. He can seize it when we get it set up on her place."

Smoothers agreed and wished him luck Slocum caught the horse, saddled it, and rode for her place. He arrived in the late afternoon and found the windmill was creaking even louder in the wind. Checking his Colt, he dismounted. No horses were in sight. Nothing stirred, and he went to the door. "Bob? You here?"

No answer. He went inside and found chairs overturned. Broken dishes were on the floor. There had been a struggle. Then, in the shadows, he saw her bed had been stripped of the blankets. He squeezed his eyes shut. There had been someone there waiting for her return. *Sumbitches*. They'd jumped her when she came inside, and no doubt they'd raped her again from the look of the bedsheets.

Anger made him see red. He walked to the door and pounded the facing with his fist. Where had they taken her? Every hour that ticked by, she was receiving more of their abuse. He had to find her and quickly. He'd known a woman who the Comanche had raped over and over—she'd lost her mind and was never right again. Just sat in a rocker on the porch, reliving the horror even when she was awake.

"Don't rape me! Don't rape me!" she would scream until someone came outside to comfort her and tell her it was all right. That the danger for her was over. But she would be trembling by then and beside herself.

"I saw 'em. I saw 'em, they was coming for me. They had dicks big as horses. You won't believe me, but I swear they're three foot long, too."

She embarrassed her poor husband with her ranting, but nothing could be done for her. Doctors told him her mind was locked on that incident. Her two young daughters cared for her, and the beautiful woman lived in her own world, rocking away her days humming a tuneless song.

Outside the ranch house, Slocum began searching the dust for tracks, wondering if that poor woman had ever recovered. Probably not. He should never have let Roberta come back here by herself. If anything more had happened to her, he'd have to take the blame.

The prints of three horses left the yard. *Damnit. I'm coming, girl.*

Chapter 7

The shadows grew longer and the trail dimmer. The horses he was tracking were headed back toward Antelope Springs. Soon he'd have to give up tracking and ride in there hoping to find someone who had seen her with them. He set in loping the horse, trying to figure out why they had taken her with them. Maybe as a hostage. Somehow, he had to find her, and the job wouldn't be easy without tracks or some idea where she could be. If he could find those deputies, maybe he could separate them and get the truth out of one of them.

Phelps would be the tough egg to crack, but as mad as Slocum felt over the kidnapping, he could get a five-page confession out of him, too. It was late when he left the horse at the livery and spoke to the hostler.

"You know Miss Bakker?"

"Yeah, what about her?"

"You seen her in town tonight?"

The man shook his head in the lantern light. "Not to-night."

"You seen Phelps around tonight?"

"No, not tonight. You need him?"

"No, I can find him when I do."

"Sure, sure, mister."

Slocum left the livery and went several doors down. He slipped in between the saddlery and the laundry. He watched the livery doors, and in minutes the hostler came out into the starlit street and looked all around. Then, with a hitch in his walk, he hurried up the street.

In the deep shadows, Slocum shook his head. He'd suspected from the way the man had acted when he questioned him that he was one of the deputies' snitches. From Slocum's hideout, he watched the man hobble along on the boardwalk, clunking a bad foot on the hollow walkway. When the hostler was past him, Slocum slipped out and began to shadow him down the street from the opposite side.

When the man disappeared inside the lighted doorway of the jail, Slocum hurried across the street and slipped into the space between the jail and a dark store.

"Where's Phelps?"

"He ain't here."

"Where's he at?"

"His place, I guess. What the hell do you need him for this time of night?"

"None of your damn business." The hostler appeared in the doorway and then he crossed the street, obviously headed for Phelps's place. Slocum found himself smiling— the man might lead him to Roberta.

Concealed in the dark space, he allowed two drunks to come by him. They were slurring their words and holding each other up as they staggered by. Then, satisfied that no one was looking out the jail's front door, he set in to follow the crippled liveryman. The job of tailing him wasn't hard—but Slocum had to hiss off some town dogs. And he added some rocks to speed their way back to the safety of the buildings. Several houses lined the road, but they were merely dark shapes in the night.

Then the man disappeared from the road, and Slocum listened in the night for any sound of him. He must have left the street. In haste, Slocum crossed over, and managed to spot him moving through a grove of cottonwoods. There was a steep slope to maneuver down. How had the cripple managed to go down it? No telling.

As he moved through the deep shadows, Slocum heard some hard knocking.

"Phelps? Phelps? You better get up. I've got something you need to know." The man was coughing and heaving for breath.

"Who in the hell is it?"

"Johnny. Johnny from the stables."

"Are you crazy? What's wrong?"

Phelps never turned a light on to answer the door. But Slocum could see the door was open and someone was standing there talking to "Johnny."

"There was a fella came in town a short while ago asking about that Bakker woman and you."

"What did he ask?"

"If'n I seed her or you."

"And?"

"I told him I hadn't seen none of you or her."

"Good. Did he go in a bar?"

"Can't say. I waited till he was gone and I went to the jail. Then I come down here like you told me to do if anyone showed up."

"You did good."

"Now will you tear that wanted poster up and burn it?"

"I may."

"You promised me if I kept my eye out for you and did you a big favor, you'd do that."

"All right, I will. But you better keep on looking out for me."

"I will. I will. What's that fella up to?"

"No good. You can count on that."

"You gonna need any help?"

"Naw, Johnny, I can handle him. He's just a drifting

cowboy. You go back and look after things at the livery. I'll get back to you."

"I will, Phelps. Why, I can handle that fella with my hands tied behind my back."

"Sure. Sure. See ya." Then Phelps closed the door, and Johnny left talking to himself about Phelps tearing up the wanted poster.

Slocum eased himself behind a gnarled tree and let Johnny go by. He listened for the man's grunting going up the hill and any sound of him possibly falling down. But coughing and breathing hard, the man soon disappeared into the night. Satisfied that Johnny was gone, Slocum advanced on the jacal. There was a light on inside. Through the open window, he could see Phelps was getting dressed. Slocum felt satisfied that they hadn't brought Roberta to this location, but perhaps Phelps would lead him to her. It was what he hoped for as he squatted down in the shadows with the crickets chirping.

In a short while, Phelps came out and saddled a horse he kept in a small corral. The pony was a tail twister and it was all the man could do to keep him from bucking. They danced around sideways making passes in front of the jacal before Phelps could get him to leave. The air was hot with the man's profanity, but he soon rode out of hearing.

Slocum walked back to town. Took a room in the small hotel and slept a few hours. In the predawn, he sat on a chair in the kitchen of Gloria Hansen's Café, cradling a cup of fresh hot coffee and watching her slice smoked ham. The aroma was good. He'd already explained to her about Roberta's earlier rape and her disappearance from the ranch.

Gloria talked in a low voice though the café itself was still dark and empty, "Where do you think they have her?"

"I'm going to track down where Phelps went last night."

"Be careful. Oh, that poor girl and those bastards. Someone needs to kill the whole lot of them."

"You have no idea where they might be hiding her?"

She swept a fallen lock away from her red face with the back of her hand, and then stretched her back with a wince. "No idea, but I have my sources, too. I'll find out in case you don't."

"Good."

"Next time you need a place to sleep or hide out, use my place. First street you come to from the east. Coming in from her place. Go right, count three houses, and mine is the fourth one on the right." She shook her head and smiled. "Ain't fancy, but there ain't any bugs."

"I'll remember that."

A frown wrinkled her forehead. "Wonder what Johnny's wanted for."

"No idea."

"That damn Phelps made a pass at me once. Must have been horny. I was cleaning up late that evening, and he came in the kitchen chewing on a straw like God's answer to women.

"He came strolling over where I was and caught my arm. Jerked me around and said, 'I'm ready for some.' I picked up a butcher knife with my other hand and shoved it to his throat.

" 'So am I,' I said. 'Fried mountain oysters. Yours, I presume.'

"He let go of me and I pushed him out the back door at knifepoint. He ain't been back since." She laughed and set the long sharp knife down. "I may not be the Queen of Sheba. But I don't have to bed down with the likes of him."

"Gloria, learn what you can, but be careful. I fear they'll be more dangerous in the days ahead."

She nodded and bent over to check on her biscuits in the oven. With a towel for a holder, she removed the large pan and placed it on the range top. "Have some biscuits and butter. I'll fry you some ham and make some eggs. When did you eat last?"

"Oh, noon yesterday."

"I thought so." She fished out three large brown-top biscuits with a fork and handed them to him on a plate. "Go out at the counter and eat. I hear Josie coming. She can do the cooking now. I'll light some lamps and we'll be open."

The older woman under a shawl nodded to him. "Morning."

"This is Slocum, Bob's cowboy. Whip him up some ham and eggs."

"I can do that. Nice to meet you, sir." She hung up her shawl.

"My pleasure," he said. Then Gloria herded him out into the café. As he tasted the hot bread and she lit the lamps, gritty soles began to shuffle on the boardwalk out front, along with sleepy voices.

"Come in, guys, coffee's made," said Gloria.

An assortment of workers filed in, taking seats at the counter and at tables. Gloria began delivering cups, packing a coffeepot in the other hand. Her cheerful voice welcomed the crowd as she sashayed around the room.

She passed Slocum once and refilled his cup. "Find her," she said. "I'll be praying for the two of you."

He acknowledged her soft-spoken words. The eggs and ham and more biscuits came. He feasted, and left fifty cents by the plate, knowing full well Gloria would turn him down if he went to pay. With a wave of good-bye, he left the crowd of men who were talking and eating the food she delivered.

From the front doorway, he saw the rawboned woman staring with a serious look at him. She'd be worried until he recovered Roberta. He went to the stables, and Johnny wasn't around.

A gray-whiskered man inside took his two bits and spat tobacco. "Might rain today. My rheumatism was bad last night."

"I guess we'll see." Slocum checked the sky when he went outside. Only a fool predicted rain in this country. He rechecked the girth and swung aboard. In a few minutes, he was in the cottonwoods near Phelps's jacal. No horses were in the corral. Meant Phelps must not have came back—Slocum would have to be careful and not run into him returning. Not that he feared the man, but it might push his hand. Getting Roberta out of his clutches came first. Then he'd settle with him.

The tracks of the horse in the yard were distinct. His right front hoof made a slight twist. Plus he was shod, so the tracks stood out. Phelps had ridden south off into the real desert. Saguaros began to appear when the road dropped off the ridge into a lower elevation. Towering cactus plants, catclaw, mesquite, cholla, and beds of pancake cactus soon replaced the juniper and grass country. The country grew rougher. Volcanic rock and sharp chasms sliced the landscape. To his right, the tall range of mountains fled southward, while the main stage road wiggled off the heights he rode down.

The road carried no traffic, and he found where Phelps had taken a dim side trail with two ruts cutting the dry short foxtail grass. He looked at the broken country ahead. It soon fell off into a wide sandy dry wash, and there were signs that wagons and single horses had come and gone on this road in the past few days.

Every quarter mile, he stopped his horse and listened. In the confinement of the dry wash, he didn't want to run into Phelps. A mile farther on, the road climbed out and went up a steep hillside. Once on top, he stopped the horse and let him catch his wind. He caught sight of some horses grazing down the long grassy slope.

He dug his telescope out of the saddlebags and scoped the area. In the eyepiece, he found some corrals, and then a jacal back in the lacy mesquite to the left of the large brown-grass meadow. Time to ditch his horse somewhere and advance on foot. There was no activity around the place. He collapsed the brass scope and put it away, then rode the horse off into the chaparral and down into a dry wash out of sight.

He dismounted, loosened the cinch, and used the lariat to tie the horse. He might need to leave there in a hurry—so he left the horse saddled and on a short tie so he didn't get into any mischief. Then, wishing he had a rifle, he climbed up and began to skirt the clearing. Not having a long-range weapon always put someone at a disadvantage when scouting something out.

He came in behind the corrals and spotted a saddled horse in the pen. It must be Phelps's bronc. Good, he must still be here. But who else was here? He eased around the pen to get closer to house, the .44 in his fist. At the back of the jacal, he tried to listen. He could hear someone coughing, but wasn't certain who it was.

There was no one outside to slip up on him. Making each footfall soft, he worked his way around the eroded outside of the jacal with the adobe bricks exposed. It must have been an abandoned homestead. He paused at the corner, switched hands with revolver, and dried his right palm on the side of his pants.

He slipped around to the front, his back to the wall. The window was open and he could hear two men talking.

"Juarez will be here in two days to get her." It was Phelps's voice. "Go easy on the laudanum you give her. He only pays for good stuff."

"You bringing him up here?"

"Yeah, have her all cleaned up and that dress on her."

"I understand, Boss."

"She's worth three hundred in gold. Them Messikins really like that white pussy."

"She won't get away. I promise."

"Good. I've got to get back and find out what that damned Slocum is up to. You just be sure you don't lose her."

"You say you knew him from Kansas?"

"Yeah, we had a slick deal going up there. We let them cowboys drive them cattle up there from Texas, then sixty miles or so south of Newton, we rustled 'em, sold 'em, and made all the money." Phelps's laughter made Slocum's jaw muscles tighten.

"What did you do with the cowboys?"

"Killed 'em, of course."

"What happened?"

"Slocum and his bunch jumped us one night in camp. Cut down Jake McKay, Max Miller, and got Hash Smith, the boss, and two others that him and his vigilantes hung. I barely got away."

"He must be tough."

Slocum stopped listening. He retreated into the brush and skirted the corral. That was where he knew Phelps from—Kansas. That no-good bunch of rustlers had sent his best friend Carl Dabbs to the grave along with six of his hands. Now Slocum hid in the chaparral and let Phelps fight with his broncy horse and ride off. There'd be plenty of time later to round up his worthless hide.

If they had Roberta doped up, Slocum would have real problems getting her out of there. Those worthless bastards—they all needed to be hung. He watched the short fat man come outside and look around. Then the man pissed a big golden stream in the bright sunshine, then went back inside.

Slocum closed in on the house. He knew the interior would be dark and his eyes wouldn't be adjusted, so he needed to move quickly when he made his assault on the jacal. The .44 was cocked and ready. He needed to be certain he didn't shoot her, too.

He came through the door. "Don't move," he said.

The man scrambled for something and Slocum shot him in the back. The room boiled with eye-stinging gun smoke. The kidnapper was down, and Slocum kicked his gun on the floor across the room.

"I'm—I'm dying."

"Die hard, you sumbitch." Slocum knelt by the bed and looked at Roberta's naked figure sprawled on her back. Her hands and feet were tied.

"Don't rape me," she mumbled, and then she coughed on the smoke.

"It's me. Slocum." He cut loose her binds with his jack-knife.

"I'm dying, I'm dying," the outlaw screamed.

"Die, I don't give a damn." Slocum lifted her up. But she was limp in his arms and still mumbling, "Don't rape me again."

He hugged her. She felt like a rag doll. Where were her clothes? Best to take her outside. This gun smoke was bad and not getting better.

With a blanket he snatched off the bed, he swept her up in his arms and carried her through the open doorway. Under a mesquite, he spread the blanket as well as he could and laid her on it.

"I'll be right back," he told her, and went inside to search for her clothes. All he found was a dress. It must have been the one Phelps talked about. Where were her other clothes? He'd need to go back inside and look some more.

"Bob, can you hear me?" he asked, kneeling beside her.

"Yes."

"Where did they put your clothes?"

"They took them from me—that first night—I don't know."

"Can you sit up?"

"I feel very drunk."

"You are. They've been doping you." He pulled her up to a sitting position. Her snowy breasts were shining in the sunlight. With his hand, he swept the hair back from her face. Then he began to dress her. It wasn't easy, but at least she would be covered when she stood. The dress would fall and cover her bare legs and butt.

"They pinched my nose to make me swallow it, too," she said.

"We need to get out of here." No way that she could sit a horse.

With both hands braced behind her, she made the effort. "I can try."

"Bob, I have to go get my horse and I'll be right back. That bum in there won't ever hurt you again. You're safe now." He considered the dress. It was the best he could do under the circumstances. "You'll have to wear this till we can find better."

"I never wear a dress."

"Today you do." He rose to his knees.

"How will we get out of here?"

He kissed her. She smiled. "I know you must have taken a big risk—oh, I'm dizzy."

"Put your hands on my shoulder and I'll button the rest of it." He fumbled and she teetered, so he laid her down and finished buttoning the front of the dress with her on her back on the blanket.

"I'm so weak. I'm sorry." She looked ready to cry.

"You lie here. I'm going for the pony. I'll be right back."

Her hand clasped his arm. "Please, please don't leave me."

"Just to get the horse." No use. He'd have to carry her there.

He picked her up in his arms, the blanket wadded around her, then rose and started for the far end of the open ground. It was a long ways, and he stopped several times to kneel and rest. When he reached the horse, he set her down with her back to a rock and tightened the cinch on the animal.

She was almost asleep again. Carrying her, he led the pony to another rock so he could step up on the animal with her in his arms. No way she could ride in front of him as limp as she was.

He set out. It would be a long ride back. On the road, a man in a buckboard came past him and stopped.

"That woman of yours dying?" the gray-haired man in his forties asked. He was wearing a new felt hat and suit.

"She's pretty bad off," Slocum said.

"Get her in here. I'll tie that horse on behind." The man tied his team off and jumped down.

Slocum dismounted, and the stranger took the horse's reins.

"Is she alive?"

"Yes, it's a long story. I'll tell you on the way to town."

"Good. My name's Jeff Harte. I own the Lone Star Ranch. We can shake hands later."

"Slocum's mine. Her name is Roberta Bakker. Everyone calls her Bob. She owns the B7 Ranch and was kidnapped two days ago. They fed her laudanum and planned to sell her to some Mexican whorehouse."

"Who in the hell are *they*?"

"A deputy named Phelps and two more deputies, Carson and Yodder. There was one more of them. He's up there dying where I shot him."

"He deserves it. I've never liked that Phelps since Gantry hired him. He the leader?"

"I think so, but I can't prove much about them, except that I took her away from their man at an abandoned house back there."

"What will we do with her? Take her to the doc?"

"No, we can't risk them finding out she's all right. If we can skirt around town and no one sees us, she has a friend named Gloria Hansen and she'll be safe with her."

"The woman that runs the café?"

"Yes, that's her."

"We won't get there till dark and I know a back way. How else can I help? She's a pretty woman—hell, not much more than a kid. Those lousy no-accounts need to pay for this."

"How well do you know Gantry?"

"I donated to his campaign. Why?"

"I don't trust him. He works for Charles Worthington and that man is up to no good."

"Hmm, you think so?"

"I'm certain I brought in two rustlers who were using a running iron on one of her yearlings. They confessed that they were working for Worthington. Gantry turned them loose."

"Aw, the hell you say?"

"Mister, they been working over lots of brands in this country."

Harte clucked to the horses and then he frowned at Slocum. "The Stockmen's Association won't stand for that."

"Stockmen or no stockmen, he turned them loose. I guess by now they're in Utah or California."

"I can help you there. The chief brand inspector in Prescott also works as a range detective. I'll have him here in a few days. He'll be certain the law is enforced."

"She wrote the governor asking for his intervention. They railroaded her brother."

"Why don't I know about all this?"

"Fear. They have everyone so afraid they won't say a word. They had a special trial for her brother. Lasted two hours, she told me—the judge came in that morning, left at noon—on the day after his arrest on some trumped-up charges of stealing some of Worthington's horses."

"No one protested or did a thing?"

"She wrote the governor a letter 'cause there was no one else to turn to."

"Hell, I'll wire him when we get there."

"She didn't think they'd let her send it. In fact, she didn't trust the post office either."

He shifted her in his arms and she opened her eyes in slits. "Where—are—we?"

"Easy, Bob, we're in Mr. Harte's buckboard headed for Gloria's."

"They won't find me there?" she asked in a mumble.

"No, they won't. Go to sleep. You're safe."

"I—can't stay awake."

"You're safe."

Harte glanced over at her with an angry scowl. "They need to be hung."

"Hanging might not be good enough for them." Slocum looked at the saguaros on the hillside. Maybe stick one of them up their ass.

"What else can I do?" Harte asked.

"You can try to wire the governor to send some U.S. marshals down here. Tell him there's anarchy going on. I'll bet he never gets the wire. Don't turn your back on them. If they feel cornered, they'll shoot their way out of this. Phelps was once in a gang up in Kansas that murdered the drovers and stole their herds. We got all of them but him."

"Murdered drovers?"

"Yes. The whole crew, shot them, or cut their throats in their bedrolls, and then stole the cattle herd just days out of Newton and sold 'em."

"And they planned to sell this woman to a Mexican whorehouse."

"And even before that, three of them raped her at the ranch the day they shipped her brother off to prison."

"What did Gantry do about it?"

"Nothing."

"Well, son of a bitch, this has me upset."

"Join the crowd. She hired a well driller up in Bar-lowville to drill her a deep well. Gantry served the man a court order to stop moving the rig toward her ranch."

"On what grounds?"

"Some fictitious store owner said the well driller owed him money."

"Did they stop?"

"They're still moving it unless Gantry went back to stop 'em."

Harte reined in at the top of the grade to let his team catch their breath. "How did you get hooked in on all this?"

"A week ago, my horse colicked bad and I had to destroy him. I walked all night packing my saddle looking for some help. I arrived thirty minutes after the rapists rode out from her place."

Harte shook his head. "A helluva deal."

"That's right." He shifted her in his arms and she moaned. A helluva deal wasn't the half of it all.

Chapter 8

They arrived after dark at Gloria's. Slocum was glad a light was on and she was home. She came rushing out when she saw him carrying Roberta in his arms headed for her house.

"What happened?"

"They were drugging her at some abandoned shack. She's had a lot of laudanum. Maybe a doc should see her, but we can't let Phelps know."

Gloria shook her head. "Doc Burns is an old drunk. We better not use him. He'd blabber it all over town when he got in the bottle."

"You know Jeff Harte?"

"Yes. Good to see you. Are you helping?" She led them inside and pointed at the bed.

"I was just the driver today," said Harte.

When Roberta was out of his stiff arms and safe on the bed at last, Slocum stood back and flexed his sore limbs. "She needs to let that dope wear off. She also needs to eat. She'll have a helluva headache when she comes out of it. And she may hallucinate. Act out of her head. Is there someone can stay with her?"

"Yes, I can get someone during the day," said Gloria.

"What about a guard for her?" Harte asked.

"Good idea. But he'd have to be tough as nails if they learn she's here, and he can't be one of Gantry's men."

"Where does Sam Kent live?" Harte asked Gloria.

Busy with a wet cloth washing Roberta's face, Gloria looked up. "Down by the creek. He'd make a good one."

"He's a tough old man who use to ride shotgun on the stage," Harte explained to Slocum.

"How much will he cost?" Slocum asked.

Harte waved him off. "I'll hire him."

"She wants you," Gloria told Slocum.

He knelt down and squeezed Roberta's hand. "You'll be safe here, Bob. You'll have a guard and I'm going after Phelps."

She nodded. "Thanks—I know you risked your life for me. But I felt safer in your arms. Be careful." Then she forced a smile on her pale face and squeezed his fingers.

"Rest. Get your strength back."

"I will."

Slocum rose and spoke to Harte. "If you can manage guarding her, I need to go and check on the well-drilling crew."

"I can handle this. What about Phelps?" Harte asked.

"I have a notion he may be out at the ranch trying to stop the drilling. You make sure they don't harm her. I'll be back in a day. Try and send that message out to the governor."

"I'll do that. You think they're—" He lowered his voice. "Attacking the drill crew?"

Slocum nodded. If the writ didn't stop them, they'd use force and Phelps would be in charge of that.

Gloria handed him a cup of coffee and a cold burrito full of meat and beans. "Sorry it isn't hot, but you needed some food."

He thanked her. It would help. After his quick meal, he left Harte and Gloria to tend to Roberta and rode for the ranch. Pushing the pony hard, he planned to switch mounts at the ranch and ride a fresh one to the rig.

Coming off the steep hill in the cool predawn, he flushed quail dusting in the road. No sign of anyone around the place. At the mill, he stripped off latigos, jerked off the saddle and wet pads, then turned the pony into the lot. They still had hay in the bunker and water in the tank. Then he went with the lariat in his hand to catch Baldy.

His second loop went over his ears and the horse stopped. Outside the pen, Slocum saddled him, led him to the house, lit a lamp, and checked things. The room looked like it did the last time—messed up. Satisfied, he went out and rode north on the spunky cow horse.

The sound of gunshots came from ahead. He heard the pop of them. Was he too late? He set Baldy hard off in that direction and when he came over the next rise, he slid him to a stop. From there, he could see the drill rig and the shooters that were on some high ground to his left. Gun smoke marked the places in the large boulders the attackers were firing from.

Sporadic firing came from the drill rig, too. He reined Baldy up a draw, regretting again that he had no rifle. In a rush, he headed Baldy westward, hoping not to attract the shooters. When he saw their horses standing hip-shot in the wash, he knew what to do. Gather their ponies and put them afoot—that might unnerve them enough to surrender.

He hit the sandy floor of the wash on his boot heels in a run. Hitching bridle reins to tails, in minutes he was back aboard Baldy and leaving the wash with four horses in tow.

"Hey—our horses. They're stealing them." And the fruitless pop of pistol shots were behind him as he topped the ridge and swung east for the rig.

"Hold your fire!" he shouted when he came into view of the rig. To his relief, he could see Smoothers and Haney and the others looking haggard but alive.

He slid to a halt. "Get these ponies out of here."

The two Mexican boys took the horses and led them away from the rig and into another wash.

"That their horses?" Haney asked, out of breath.

"Yes. How long have they been shooting at you?"

"Oh, since last night," Smoothers said. "That damn Phelps rode down yesterday afternoon and told us he was taking over the rig. We didn't see it that way."

Slocum nodded. "What happened next?"

"Dan got the drop on him and we sent the four of them packing. They didn't go far, got their rifles and opened up on us."

Slocum looked off in the direction of the rocks. "I only counted three shooters left up there."

Smoothers nodded. "Good. You brung four horses so they've never sent no one for help. There were four of them when that cocky damn deputy rode in."

"Phelps?"

Dan nodded from where he was stationed with a rifle near the boiler. "It was him all right, told us he was taking over."

Two rifle shots ricocheted off the boiler and sent everyone behind it.

"They ain't the best shots, thank God," Smoothers said. "What did you get into?"

"They'd kidnapped Bob and I had to get her back."

"What?" Smoothers and Haney blinked at him in shock.

He explained to them about the whole ordeal of rescuing her and how she was in safe hands with Harte and Gloria in town.

"That damn Phelps been busy, ain't he?" Smoothers said. "He needs his neck stretched by hemp."

"Wouldn't hurt. Let me try something." Slocum cupped his hands and shouted. "You can surrender now or to the posse coming from town."

"Fuck you."

"If you surrender now, we'll make certain that posse don't lynch you."

"There ain't no posse coming."

"Phelps, your buddy at that abandoned shack is dead by this time. She's safe. You better believe there's a posse coming."

"That you, Slocum?"

"Yeah, I followed you to that shack by the meadow and after you left, your short friend made a move for a gun and it cost him his life."

"You're lying."

"No, I ain't. She's in safe hands. The law's fixing to change around here, Phelps. You're on the outside."

"We're coming out. I don't know about him, but me and Manley's giving up." It was Dawson, the lanky rustler, who appeared in the open with his hands high.

"Hold your fire," Slocum said. "Where's the fourth one?"

"Dying," Dawson said, reaching out to touch a large boulder to keep his balance climbing out. "He's gut-shot."

"Who is it?" Slocum shouted

"Johnny from the livery."

"Guess he did his last favor for you, huh, Phelps?" Slocum asked.

"Shut up. I'm coming."

"Phelps had him blackmailed over a wanted poster," Slocum said, turning to the others.

"Real handy guy," Smoothers said. He and Dan, with rifles leveled, started for the three men with their hands raised.

"Land sakes, I figured we was gone gooses," Zeke said, crawling out from under the rig with a single-shot rifle. "When's the posse gonna get here?"

"There ain't one coming." Slocum laughed.

Zeke readjusted his overall suspenders and blinked in disbelief. "There ain't one coming?"

"No."

A frown appeared on Zeke's beard-stubbled face, and then he blinked as if absorbing it all. "Well, my God, you coulda fooled me."

Then they both laughed.

When the three prisoners were in their own handcuffs and chains, they sat on the ground under guard. The two Mexicans and Dan went for the wounded man. Slocum left Smoothers in charge of the prisoners so he and Haney could go scout the site of the well. It needed to be drilled in a place so they could use the tank for a reservoir.

They rode over and studied the site from the high point. Slocum used his hand to show the area Haney needed to set up on. Then they went down to the dam.

"If we can hit artesian water here, she'll have the setup to irrigate maybe a hundred acres." Slocum indicated to Haney the available farmland below there.

Haney nodded. "It would make a wonderful farm. You sure she's going be all right?"

"Oh, yes, she has a strong constitution."

"I've been worried ever since she left that morning. She's a wonderful person."

"Good, let's get her a well."

"Depends what we hit down there, but in a few weeks we should know."

"Can we sled that rig in above this tank?"

"I guess we could sled it anywhere after the trip here." He gave Slocum a smug grin.

"What about fuel?"

"I'll need some coal."

"I'll bet Smoothers has a pile of slabs."

"It really needs coal for it to work right. There's a coal mine above Barlowville. It's got a lot of rock in it, but I was going to use it for the well I'd planned to drill at the mine."

"How much does coal cost?"

"Five dollars a ton here."

"How long will it last?"

"Oh, a ton will last two days."

"We better order three loads and then a load every second day."

Haney made a worried face. "They might not be able to mine that much."

"Get your order in. See what they can do."

Haney agreed, and they walked over the ground they needed to pull the rig across.

"It sure needs some leveling." Haney pointed out the places that were too steep.

"Send Zeke up to the ranch and get the scraper. I saw one up there. With Smoothers' team, he can level this in half a day."

Haney nodded. "What're you going to do with the prisoners?"

"Keep them around until we hear from the governor." Nothing else he could do with them—loose, they'd sure run to warn Worthington and Gantry.

"Don't you figure that the sheriff will come out here and check on them?"

"He does, he can wait in irons for the governor's action here, too."

Haney's face paled some under the bright sun. "But—but—ain't he the chief lawman in the county?"

"Haney, when I get through with him, I'm damn sure he won't be sheriff."

"You sure that she's going to be all right?"

"Bob'll be fine. They tried to kill her."

Haney took off his hat and scratched his brown hair. "Lots in this world I don't know, but I'm sure learning quick. Don't guess I'd stand a chance at it, but I'd sure like to court her when she gets well."

"You better do that then."

Haney blinked his eyes in disbelief. "You serious?"

"All she can say is no."

"Oh, that would stab my heart."

"Yeah, well, you have to get stabbed a few times in life, too."

"I'll remember that."

Slocum went to Smoothers and they squatted on their heels to talk. Slocum told him about holding the prisoners and why. The wounded one would go to his reward before sundown—gut-shot, a doc couldn't save him. They'd found some whiskey in the other prisoners' things and that had eased him some.

"You watch Phelps. He's escaped tougher deals than this before, and I imagine that broody bastard over there is hatching a plan right now to do just that."

"We'll guard 'em."

"I imagine you need to get back to your sawmill?"

"We will when we get this settled."

"Haney's sending Zeke for the scraper," Slocum said. "And I'm going back to town and see what's happening. Keep your guard up. Worthington learns we've got them, he might bring an army down on us."

"Yeah, Zeke just took my wagon and the two Mexicans to help load it. You be careful in town. And check on her, too. We'll be set up over there drilling when you get back." Smoothers looked as concerned as Slocum had ever seen him.

"Good. That's where I'm going first—to see about her. It'll be dark by the time I get there, so I'll have some cover."

Smoothers gave a scowl at the seated prisoners. "How long before you hear from the governor, do you reckon?"

"That I don't know."

Smoothers sucked on an eyetooth. "We might get plumb tired of them."

"Don't lynch 'em. That don't solve a thing. I'll be back."

Smoothers rose stiffly. "Bring some good whiskey back, my good stuff's about gone."

With a grin, Slocum clapped him on the shoulder. "I'll do that."

He'd do lots more, too. Better get to town and see about Roberta and what was happening there. In long strides, he left Smoothers and headed for Baldy—he checked the sun. Past midday. It would be late when he got there.

Chapter 9

In the middle of the night, a quarter moon hung over the sawtoothed hills to the west. Slocum had ridden by starlight, and Baldy signaled growing weary by short snorts in the dust as they approached the dark town. To not let anyone know about his arrival, he came in the wide way to Gloria's place.

He dismounted behind her shack, wondering if Harte's man was guarding the place. Aside from the crickets creaking, nothing was out of place when he tied Baldy to a mesquite tree limb. Listening for sounds, he loosened the wet latigos—nothing. Gun in hand, he started for the shack.

Then his world went dark and he remembered falling facedown. He'd lost his hat in the blow, and recalled smelling the acrid dirt when he came to lying on his belly—his wrists behind his back were in irons. Who hit him? Gantry? Or someone else?

"Get up slow," Gantry said. "You're under arrest for murder."

"Who did I kill?"

"Someone in Kansas, the poster said. I wired 'em. They have two deputies coming for you."

"Where's Bob and Gloria?"

"I don't know—they weren't here when I got here."

"You know your deputy Phelps kidnapped Bob and took her down south to some old shack and planned to sell her to some Mexican slavers."

Gantry shoved him out in front of the starlit shack. "Stay there."

The lawman got his horse and came back with it. "That's another damn lie about my deputy. Who's going to believe a wanted man that Kansas is willing to come after?"

"Anything's happened to Bob and you'll pay for it."

The lawman laughed aloud. "When? When you get out of jail?"

"You can think it's funny now. Better get it all in, 'cause you won't laugh later."

Gantry caught him by the arm. "Listen, you troublemaking sumbitch, I may not have to give you to them deputies. I can show them your corpse and collect my five hundred bucks reward."

"They won't pay it. You ain't the first one they suckered in on that reward deal. They never pay it."

"They better or they won't get your ass."

Slocum shrugged as he walked along to his own horse. "Tell them to wire the money then—they won't."

"Why not?"

"They never have." He looked at the star-pricked sky. He had Gantry on the right string. All he needed to do was pull it some more. "There must be half a dozen folks across the country still waiting for their reward money."

"Shut up, you're making me mad."

They headed toward town. Slocum was bareheaded and walking ahead of Gantry, who led both horses. The cuffs cut into his wrists they were on so tight. Not much he could do but go along. There'd be chances later on for him to escape.

Where had Harte and the women gone?

When he was locked in the cell by himself and Gantry

was gone, he used the bunk to sleep, hoping his sore head would quit throbbing. The day's heat made the jail sweltering when voices woke him. It was Worthington and Gantry arguing about something. Slocum pretended to sleep and listened.

"What's your deputy got done on the other situation?"

"He's got the drill rig in his custody."

"You know that for damn certain?"

"Sure. If not, he'd send me word. Phelps is a good man. I keep telling you that."

"All right. Where are those damn women?"

"Hell, I don't know," Gantry said, sounding disgusted he'd even ask him. "They took a powder."

"Does Slocum know anything?"

"Naw, he expected to find them there, too."

"Somebody knows. Somebody knows right where they are." Worthington began to pace the jail's dirt floor, squeezing his chin.

"Well, I'll be fucked if I know." Gantry dropped in his wooden swivel chair, and it protested when he leaned back. "They've got to be somewhere."

"Brilliant. Brilliant. Hell, everyone has to be somewhere, even corpses in the cemetery. It's *where* they are that we need to know."

"I'll put out some feelers. Damn café's closed. Has everyone asking questions and pissed off. That dumb old Mexican cook at the saloon cooks everything with too much hot peppers. Nobody likes his slop."

"Probably does that so he don't have to cook so much."

"Yeah, that's probably why he uses them."

"You going to check on Phelps today?" Worthington asked.

"I told you, I'd've heard if he'd had any problems."

"Wish I was that damn sure. We've got to find the women."

"Hell, I don't know where to start."

"Damnit, Gantry, you got as much to lose as I have. Find 'em." Worthington stomped out the door.

Gantry shook his head and walked over to the cell that Slocum was in. He looked around to be certain they were alone. "I wired them bastards in Kansas for my money."

Slocum, acting sleepy, raised up. "What did they say?"

"I ain't heard yet."

Slocum nodded, lay back down, and acted like he was going to sleep.

"Them bastards want you—they better send the money."

"They won't," he mumbled after the sheriff.

"Joe's bringing you some food from the saloon. Don't try nothing. He's got orders to shoot to kill."

"Sure." Gantry was leaving. Might be his chance to escape, depending on how tough the guard was. He closed his eyes and slept some more.

"Wake up. I got your food."

Slocum raised up and looked at the white-whiskered tray holder. The man held the tray and fumbled with keys, using the barred door to hold up one side of the tray until the lock finally clicked. He fought trying to open the door, and at last had it back and started into the cell. "Here's your meal."

Slocum jumped up, reached over the food, caught him by the vest, and dumped food and all down his front. He slammed the man hard against the bars, then swept the six-gun out of his holster.

"I—I—" the man stuttered.

"I'm not going to kill you. Shut up."

"I will. I promise."

"Get over on that bunk. One yell out of you and you're dead."

The man tripped and fell down, then scrambled on the bed. By then Slocum had the cell door locked, and tossed the keys on the desk. He took a .44/40 Winchester off the rack, and searched through the drawer till he found rounds for it. Jamming cartridges into it, he kept an ear open for any sounds. When the rifle was loaded, he pocketed several extra shells in his vest.

The livery was half a block away. Not many in the town knew him on sight or knew he was in jail unless Gantry had told them. Slocum would sure need Baldy, and Gantry'd left him at the livery. Carrying the rifle against his leg and the old man's Colt in his waistband, he started for the stables. The sign shone in the sun. It looked like a long way away. His boots rumbled on the boardwalk as he passed several folks who never raised an eyebrow.

Then, with sweat pouring down from his armpits, he stepped into the shade of the livery. The sweet smell of alfalfa and the sourness of horse piss assailed his nose. No one came. In the aisle of the barn he discovered Baldy, still saddled, and pulled up the girths. From his location, he could see out the open doors if anyone was coming. Cinches tight, he mounted, and ducked under the rafters and rode outside into the bright light. Still no alarm. He turned Baldy east—the skin crawled on the back of his neck. Then, in a short lope, he left town.

On the rise, he stopped and looked back. It might be a trap. His escape had been too simple—too easy. No sign of any pursuit. Still, he wasn't satisfied. His head had begun to pound again. It damn sure wouldn't be a good day despite his "release from custody."

At the crossroads, he took the left-hand road to Barlowville. Somewhere up in those hills ahead, he'd wait and jump anyone riding up his back trail, if there was somebody back there. The women's safety niggled at him, but Gantry couldn't find them, or so he said. With Phelps in irons, they must be safe. He certainly hoped so.

In a dry wash, he waited over an hour by sun time and no one came by. So he remounted Baldy and cut across country to the ranch. It was well past sundown when he got there. No one was around the place. He switched horses and headed for the drill camp.

When he drew near, he could hear the steam engine running and the pounding of the drill. There was lantern light at the rig. He dismounted. Haney waved at him with his free hand. With the other hand on the cable, he was feeling each pound to be certain that his drill didn't wedge in the rocks and break off the cable. If it became stuck, he had to clutch the cable or lose it.

"How's it going?" Slocum asked.

"Fine, we're already down fifty feet. But I figure there's some hard rock coming soon."

"I'm going to see the Chinaman. I ain't ate in twenty-four hours."

"Why?"

"Gantry arrested me. The women are gone and I don't know what's happening."

"Women are gone?"

"I can't figured it out, but Gantry doesn't have them. Maybe Harte took them. Gantry was hiding at Gloria's, and cracked me over the head, then tossed me in jail."

"How did you get out?"

"I jumped the guard."

"Go eat. I'll shut down here in a while."

Slocum nodded and went to find the Chinaman.

"You have any food?" he asked the Celestial, who was busy sewing on something in the firelight.

"Food?"

"I haven't eaten a thing in a day."

"Oh. I fixie some."

"Good." Slocum dropped to the ground. The prisoners were sleeping across the fire from him.

"What's happened?" Smoothers said, coming in with his Winchester and setting it down to pour himself some coffee.

Slocum told him about the women being gone and his stint in the jailhouse along with his subsequently breaking out.

"Where are they—the women, I mean?"

"Harte may have taken them to his ranch."

"How are we going to find out?"

"I guess ride down there."

"Dan and I could go with you." Smoothers looked back at the prisoners. "If we didn't have them—"

"You guys need to be here and look after Haney, too, until I find the women."

Haney had shut down the drill for the night and now joined them. He dropped his butt on the ground beside them. "We can always drill. I want to go back and help you find them."

"First, you're the driller and I'm the looker."

They all three laughed, and Lo brought Slocum a plate of meat and beans.

"Thanks," Slocum said, and began to eat. Hardly realizing how famished he was, he chewed his food slowly. The meal and a few hours' sleep might replenish some of his strength.

"What next?" Smoothers asked.

"I'll try to find Harte's ranch and see what he knows about the women. I left them in his care."

The big man nodded. "So Gantry thinks his man has this place under control?"

"That's what he told Worthington." Slocum looked up from his food to grin.

"What about the governor?"

"Right now, we don't know if he even got her letter. Or if he'll do anything about it."

"So what do we need to do?"

"Find those two women. Then I'll do what I have to with the governor."

Haney nodded, then shook his head with concern in the firelight. "I sure hope they don't hurt them. I mean Bob especially."

"I'll find them. I'm sure that Worthington does not have them. Him and Gantry talked about their disappearance from Gloria's place."

"What if them Mexican slavers have 'em?"

"In two days I'll know."

In the light of the crackling fire, Haney made a face. "That's sure a long time."

"Well, if I had wings, I could do it faster."

"No. No. I mean for those women if they're captives."

Slocum agreed and finished his food. There were lots of things for him to do, and on top of that the Abbott brothers from Fort Scott, Kansas, were on their way there to pick him up. Might be that he had a week at best. Depended on where they were at when they got the word he was in jail.

His life was on a timed fuse.

Chapter 10

Two hours sleep and Slocum rode out. Harte's ranch would be the first place to check and it was somewhere south of Antelope Springs. Under the stars, he crossed the higher country studded in junipers, and by daybreak he was at a small crossroads store.

A willowy woman in a blue polka-dot dress came out and pitched a pail of mop water in the dust. She blinked at the sight of him. "You're out awfully early."

He dismounted and nodded. Without his hat, he felt naked. "Or I'm up late."

She wiped her forehead on the back of her hand and appraised him from the small porch. She was tall under the plain blue dress that hugged her fine figure. He guessed her to be thirty years old. Her brown hair was in a bun on the back of her head. Her face looked too sharp to be pretty—high cheekbones under her blue eyes, a sharp nose, and a small mouth.

She looked around as if searching to see if he'd come alone.

"Just me," he said, loosening the latigos.

"Where're you headed?"

"Jeff Harte's ranch. Am I close?"

She nodded, still acting uneasy.

"All I need is something to eat. Is there something wrong?"

She shook her head. "Come in. Come in."

He followed her inside the dark store, and she bolted the door after them. Then, with her hand on his arm, she guided him toward the rear of the business area.

"You looking for work?"

"No, I'm looking for two missing women."

She stopped him in the dimly lit aisle, still clutching his arm. "You married?"

"No, ma'am."

"Good. My name's Marie Goddard." She guided him on to the counter. Sunlight slanted inside in streams overhead as she stopped him. Her hands went around his neck and with half-closed eyes she looked up at him. "Food comes second."

He needed no more hints and kissed her. Her mouth was hungry and she pressed her body to him. Where was her man? Hell, her needs were obviously too great for him to be around.

He felt her breast through the dress and she gasped. Breaking her mouth from his, she tried to recover her breath. "Come on."

There was a double bed in the shadowy living quarters. She began unbuttoning her dress—she was serious—damn serious. He toed off his boots. When her dress was open to the camisole inside, she removed his vest and then undid his shirt as he took off his gun belt. He hung the .44 on a nearby ladder-back chair and unbuckled his belt, and she pulled off his suspenders.

Her breath came in gulps, and her smile of anticipation had to be kissed as he undid his fly and his pants fell to his knees. Forced to part his mouth from hers, he shed his britches and then swept her up in his arms.

She gave a short shriek of surprise, and then trapped his face to kiss him more. She was taller than he'd even imagined as he stepped to the bed. When she broke away from his mouth, he set her on top of the bed and she unfurled the slip over her head.

In the dim light, he could see the dark pointed nipples on her small breasts. She reached back and undid her hair, which fell below her shoulders. When she threw her head to shake loose her hair, her tits shook also.

He knelt on one knee on the bed as she reclined on her back. When he started to go beside her, she raised her knees and guided him between them.

"Don't hurt me," she said softly.

"Never."

There would be no time for foreplay between them. She wanted him—*now*.

Between her long slender legs, he reached underneath to nose his half-full erection in her gates. They were moist enough, and he eased his shaft through them and it slid inside to her ring. From his own growing excitement a great surge of blood rushed in, and his erection quickly stiffened. His shaft plunged through her constriction.

She cried out, "Oh, my God . . ." and raised her hips off the mattress to better accept him.

His butt was aching to drive his throbbing dick to her deepest depths, and they soon became entangled in an all-consuming life-and-death battle of his hard dick against her contracting pussy. His back muscles drove him in and out. Her heels beat a tattoo on the back of his calves.

Mouth open, she moaned aloud, wiggled for more of him, and then wilted when she came. With slow, steady strokes, he revived her, and in minutes she came again.

Her half-opened eyes were glazed. Her mouth was open, sucking air and making sounds of pleasure. With her hair in her face, she clutched his arms and made a hard-pressed effort to have all of him. The final cannon shot rose from his testicles and flew out the skintight head of his dick. They collapsed in each other's arms.

"How far is the Lone Star Ranch?" he asked, climbing off her.

"You looking for work?" she asked, sweeping the hair back from her face. She braced her arms behind her so her pointed breasts were exposed in the slats of light and shadows in the back room.

"No, I have business with Harte."

"Shucks," she said, scooting across the bed to sit on the edge.

"You have a man?"

"Did I act like I had a man?"

He pulled on his pants. "I couldn't tell."

"Well, I don't. He got killed three years ago. They said he broke his neck."

"They?"

"See, they came and told me about it after they buried him. Said it was too hot—told me they found him on the stage road and buried him there."

"What broke his neck?"

She shook her head. "They said his horse threw him."

"Who's they?"

"That deputy Phelps and another redheaded one."

"You doubted 'em?"

She put the camisole on over her head. Then she rose and pulled it down with a shake of her hips. "He's the law, ain't he?"

"He's wearing the badge."

Busy buttoning his shirt, he watched her closely. She wasn't telling him everything. "He make any advances at you?"

Her eyes narrowed. "Why do you ask?"

He watched her put her arms in the dress. " 'Cause he's hurt other women in the county."

"What's one more?"

Even in the shadowy room, he could see the tears in her eyes. He reached out and hugged her. "It's close to over."

Her body shook in sobs as his arms held her tight.

"I never cried when Ezra died. I never cried when he came by and used my body—I hated it. A girl should have her choice who she beds and don't. They don't have slavery anymore. Do they?"

With his hand, he swept the hair back from her face and looked down at her. "No, they don't." Then he smothered her against his chest. "Sorry I made you cry, but I needed to know that."

"No—no—I'm glad you did. I was so ashamed, I'd never told anyone. Now it's out and I feel better. Who are you anyway?"

"Just a man passing through. Two women disappeared and I hope that Harte is hiding them."

She shrugged. "I don't know. I haven't even seen one of his hands in days."

"Marie, I have to get up there and know for sure."

She caught his arm. "I have some fresh-baked bread and some butter. Before you leave, eat some of that. Plus some prickly-pear jelly. You need to eat something."

He agreed. How many more women had Phelps raped besides the two he knew about? Lots of unanswered questions about that bastard.

He struck a match for her and lit a lamp. It lighted her dry sink as well as the table and chairs. He sat down on one and pulled on his boots. She sliced off one of several brown-crusted loaves with a sharp knife, and the aroma of sourdough filled the air.

"You must think I run a house of ill repute out here." She delivered several slices of her bread on a plate along with butter in a bowl. "Knife and jam coming next and, oh, yes, coffee."

When she returned, he caught her wrist. "No, I don't think that, but sometimes a person gets so lonely they have to bust out."

She looked hard at him. "I was that way when you rode

up. Something about the look in your eye. I said to myself, 'Crazy woman, here is a man riding through your life that you need to know better.' Then I forgot all my good sense."

"Thanks." He was busy buttering the first slice.

"No. I owe you. I got that cry behind me—" She set down the two cups of coffee, swept her dress under her, and took a seat across from him. "I needed that over. But it helped. Now, who are the women you're looking for?"

"Gloria, who runs a café. I guess the only one in town. And Bob Bakker."

"I know them. Wasn't her brother found guilty of rustling?"

"A frame-up, I'm afraid."

"They can break a man's neck, I guess they can frame another."

"If I can find out anything about him, I'll let you know."

"Oh, I guess it wouldn't matter. Ezra's gone." She held the cup in both hands and shrugged her shoulders.

"It might give you closure." He was savoring the bread. It sure tasted wonderful after all the soda biscuits he'd eaten of late.

"I know it's not been long enough, but there is a man you need to meet," he said.

A suspicious look spread over her face. "Who?"

"A man who owns a sawmill. A big nice guy—a man's man. He's been helping me. Abe Smoothers is his name."

She shrugged. "I don't know him."

"You will. He'll fill that door coming through it."

"Why would he want me?"

Slocum smiled and held up the butter-and-jelly-smeared slice of bread. "This would convince him."

Her laughter rang out. "So you're a matchmaker, too?"

"Naw, but you two would have lots of fun together."

"When will he come to see me?" She chewed on her lower lip.

"When we get things settled. Maybe a few weeks."

"That could be a lifetime." She wrapped her arms around herself and shuddered, then grinned at him like his promise had excited her.

"He's worth waiting for," Slocum said.

"You're sure he'll come?"

"Yes. I have to go."

She rushed over and kissed him. "Thanks, Slocum. You're welcome here any time."

"I may need a place to rest over again."

Acting shocked, she led him to the front door. "You be careful. Wait," she said, and reached inside for a hat. It was a gray felt one. "He won't need it. You will."

It fit him and he nodded in gratitude, then headed for his horse. She followed him and, at his horse, he turned to her, set the hat on the back of his head, and kissed her. It wasn't easy leaving her for Harte's place.

The ranch lay in the bend of a large wash. Slocum could see the alfalfa plots that showed green. He descended off the mountain into the valley, and headed for the towering cottonwoods that partly concealed the main house, corrals, and outbuildings.

A few stock dogs heralded his arrival, and a cowboy armed with a rifle stepped out of a bunkhouse.

"Morning, the boss man here?"

The cowboy shook his head.

"My name's Slocum and I came to see if two women were here."

The cowboy shook his head.

"They been here?"

"Yep."

"Where did they go?"

"He said you'd be coming. Him and them women went to Prescott to see the governor. Told us to be on the look-out."

"How long have they been gone?"

"Left day before yesterday. Said it would take a week."

Slocum nodded. "Did anyone else check on them?"

"Nope, you're the first."

"Guess a man could rest here a few hours?"

"Make yourself at home. There's grain for your horse in that shed."

"I may take a bath now I know they're all right."

"Suit yourself, but it ain't Saturday night. There's a sheepherder shower behind here." He nodded in that direction.

"Good. Anyone else here?"

"The boss lady. She's up at the house, I guess."

"Fine, I won't need anything. Do I need to refill the tank?"

"Naw, the windmill will."

"You the foreman?"

"Yep."

"I never caught your name."

"Nevada."

"Thanks, Nevada."

"I don't know what for." The man walked off with his rifle in the crook of his arm.

Harte's man certainly wasn't a blabbermouth. Slocum led Baldy over and watered him at the mill tank. Then he undid the girths and took him to the shed. Inside the shed, he put some white Mexican corn in a canvas feed bag. Outside, he removed the bridle and put the bag on the horse. Then, using a rope from the shed, he hitched Baldy to the rack.

With a bar of soap and a towel from his saddlebags, he walked around to the sheepherder's shower. Two barrels overhead on a stand contained the water supply, with a pull rope on each to start the flow. The shower was behind the other buildings, and a high board fence around it offered some privacy.

He sat on a bench and took off his boots. Road weary,

he undressed slowly. Stretching the tight muscles in his back and legs, he winced in discomfort. Gun and clothing were hung on pegs. With his bare skin exposed to the mid-morning heat, he took the soap and stepped gingerly on the wooden grates. The area smelled of lye soap and the sourness of wash water as he pulled the chain.

The shock of the cold water about stopped his heart. He released the rope and shut off the flow.

"Use the other one, that's one's the freshest." It was a woman's voice behind him.

He didn't turn, though he wondered who she was. "You the boss lady?"

"I'm his sister Cora."

"Harte's?"

"His wife died three years ago."

Slocum nodded. "Excuse me. My name's Slocum. I'm taking a shower."

"I had the same idea. He told me all about you."

"That's good. Suit yourself about the bath. Plenty of room."

She laughed out loud at him. "Since you don't care, I'll take one with you."

"Fine. It's your ranch. What about Nevada?"

"He minds his own business."

He turned to look at her as the flaxen blond-headed woman stepped out of a riding skirt, showing her snowy legs in the sunlight. She never glanced over at him. Undoing the man's shirt she wore, she shed it, and he caught sight of her pear-shaped breasts. The sight of them made his stomach roil.

Then he heard hoofbeats. Several riders were coming. He rushed to his six-gun.

"Nevada can handle them. Come with me."

He scooped up all his things, and she bent over to gather her clothes and boots. Her shapely derriere looked like ice cream.

"The cellar," she whispered as the horses drew closer. In the lead, she rushed to the steps and unbarred the door.

In seconds, they were in the dark cellar's cool interior. Slocum put his ear to the door to listen. Was it some of Gantry's bunch? They were reining up, he could hear them.

She pressed, then squirmed her silky flat stomach against his bare butt, and then embedded her nipples in his back. Her small palm ran over his hips, and then she discovered his privates with her fingers. It was hard for him to pay attention.

"Harte here?" It was Gantry's voice.

He couldn't hear Nevada's reply, but his dick was fast responding to her strokes.

"Where did he go?" Gantry asked.

"Business—"

"I'm looking for an escaped prisoner."

The reply was inaudible, but her hot breath on his shoulders was loud enough. His heart was going faster.

"Tell Harte I want to see him right away when he gets back. Let's go, boys. I've got another place south of here we need to check."

They were going to the hideout where Phelps had taken Bob. Cora slipped around in front of him, stood on her toes, and kissed him. With a new grip on his tool in the cellar's darkness, she laughed. "That Gantry is dumb. I told my brother he was stupid. I think he believes me now."

She twisted around and bent over with her butt pressed against him and his pole. "We can do it here."

He closed his eyes and let her guide his erection into her cunt. That posse might be on their way to Haney and Smoothers. She lined it up and he pushed it into her. His calloused hands gripped the smooth skin that covered her slender hips to steady her.

He was enjoying every minute of their coupling, though a bed would have been a better place to enjoy her. Borrow a fresh horse—oh, her walls were contracting on his sore dick. He punched her harder. No way he could beat them back to the B7 without a fast one, but he needed to be there to help them. Her low moans of pleasure grew louder and she slapped his leg for more—faster.

Then he felt the end coming and jammed himself hard against her butt. When he came hard, she nearly fainted, and he held her up until she regained her bearings.

He turned her around, kissed her on the temple, and squeezed her. As much as he hated to leave her wonderful ass, he needed to get back to the drill rig. At least the other two women were safe in Harte's care, so he could stop worrying about them.

Chapter 11

Nevada caught him a big thoroughbred to use. The man was his same noncommittal self, and soon left them alone. Cora followed Slocum around as he saddled the horse, and slapped her heavy cord skirt with a quirt all the time while telling him about everything in her life. A lost husband whose body was never found. Her only child killed in a buggy wreck. She even opened two buttons on her shirt to show him the knot on her collarbone from that accident.

When his saddle was on the high-spirited gelding, he cinched down, dropped the stirrup, and then kissed her good-bye.

"Don't forget where I'm at," she whispered before releasing him.

"I won't. Tell Harte what Gantry is up to. I'll come by and check on him in a few days. I sure hope he convinces the governor to act. Over at the Bakker place, they're getting tired of keeping Gantry's men prisoners."

"I will, and do come back—please?"

"Things are going fast. We'll have to see."

She threw him a kiss, and he left holding the bay's head up because the horse acted ready to pitch a fit. The bay was iron-jawed and hard to contain. Finally, Slocum was

113

convinced he needed some of the edge ridden off him, and let him go. And the big horse flew in no time to Marie's store.

He dismounted, adjusted the crotch in his pants, and hitched the restless bay horse to her rack. Some airtight tomatoes would furnish him nourishment on the trail and cut the dust out of his throat.

"The fine sheriff was here asking about you," she said from the doorway, and stepped back to let him inside.

"What else is new? He came by Harte's, but I was unavailable. Him and his posse rode on south. Give me four cans of airtight tomatoes."

"Where you headed now?" She slipped behind the counter and put the tomatoes on the countertop.

"To see how my drillers are doing."

"Won't Gantry figure that out and go out there next?"

"Whatever he wants to do. I'm waiting on the governor to take some action. How much are they?"

She smiled and shook her head. "My present to you."

He slapped down a dollar. "That cover them?"

"More than enough. I owe you twenty cents change."

"I don't want you going broke taking care of wandering cowboys. I'll take a can of peaches if that twenty cents will buy them."

She put the peaches on the counter, then reached underneath and took out a cloth poke to put them in. "Come back and fill that sack again some time."

With the poke in his hand, he reached over and kissed her. "I may do that."

"Damnit, you be careful," she shouted after him as he hurried to leave.

If he stayed around there another minute or so, he'd have been in bed with her. So he left on the high-headed bay horse. Baldy was a tough mountain horse that could single-foot, but this hot-blooded gelding ate the miles up. He was approaching Roberta's ranch house right after sundown, and coming down the slope, he saw a light on in the house. And wood smoke was on the wind. His hand went to the .44 on his hip. He shifted it around.

Was someone from the drilling crew using the house? Or was there "company" waiting for him? Checking the bay, he drew up short of the house, ready for anything. A barrel-chested man came to the door. He was bareheaded.

"Been waiting for someone all afternoon. Figured they'd show up soon or later. Rex Rayburn, head brand inspector for the territory. Governor sent me down to check on things."

"Slocum's my name. You hear the drill rig?"

"Yeah, earlier, but I thought that was mining machinery. I was going to go check on it in the morning."

"It's a long story, and Miss Bakker has been, I understand, back to Prescott to talk to the governor."

"I want to hear it all. Coffee's on and I've got some grub cooking."

"Fine. After we eat, we'll go up to the drill camp and check with them. I have three men being held as prisoners up there until the law changes in Antelope Springs."

"Lord, what's the sheriff doing?"

"It's what he ain't doing that's the problem. I took two men in as rustlers, and now they must be his deputies. They got a promotion."

"Well, all I can do is enforce the brand law." Using a holder, he put a skillet of fried potatoes, onions, and bacon on the table. "Hope this will fill you some."

"It looks great. You ever hear of a man named Worthington?" Slocum asked, filling his plate while Rayburn poured their coffee.

The man shook his head.

"He came in here a few years ago. Trying to buy out all the good places. He's tried his damnedest to halt the well drilling, and I think he's behind the sheriff's attempts to stop us."

"Why's that?"

"I think there's artesian water underneath this country."

Rayburn whistled. "Oh, I see what you mean."

"Her dad set up some acres below where they could catch some water and make a small winter grain crop. But artesian water would make over a hundred acres here irrigable. Then there'd be more places in the area that could strike water and so on."

"I see. It's maybe worth two bucks an acre dry, but with free water it could be worth a hundred."

Slocum nodded, busy eating the tasty food.

After the meal, they rode up to the drill camp. Dan was armed with his rifle when he met them.

"Things going okay?" Slocum asked him. "Oh, this is the head brand inspector. Rex Rayburn, that's Dan."

The two shook hands. Then Smoothers and Haney joined them and after introductions, they all went on up to the campfire. Slocum told them about Gantry and his posse. He ended with, "I expect him to come here in the near future and check on his deputies."

"No word from the governor?" Smoothers asked.

Slocum shook his head. "Harte took Bob and Gloria to see the governor after Rex left Prescott. I think he'll send help when he hears the entire story."

"He was upset about the branding-law problems that she wrote him about," Rex said. "That's why he sent me down here."

"But you can't arrest the sheriff," Smoothers said.

"No, but a U.S. marshal or one of his deputies can."

Smoothers agreed. "He ain't sent one so far."

Rex shrugged. "You can't tell. He may be on his way."

Smoothers called for a drink, and they passed around a bottle of good whiskey.

"Then we need to send someone after supplies. We'll be eating jackrabbits next," he said.

Slocum nodded. They would need something with this many to feed. "Maybe Dan could go and I'll stay here and help guard after I show Rex some of the worked-over brands."

"He better go to Barlowville. He goes to the county seat, it might draw attention," Smoothers said.

Slocum agreed, and went for his bedroll. Haney trailed along with him. "You don't know if she—I mean Miss Bakker—is all right?"

"No, but Harte is a tough enough guy, they won't get her from him."

Haney dropped his head in defeat. "Bet he's my competition, too."

"Aw, Haney, you can't tell. How's the drilling coming?"

"We hit a trickle of water, but it isn't anything."

"How deep are you now?"

"Eighty feet."

"Where is the artesian water? How deep?"

"A hundred fifty maybe."

"Why, you're halfway."

"Wish I was that optimistic about her and getting the water."

"I bet they work out." Slocum unfurled his bedroll. "I'll get some sleep, and in the morning I'll show Rex some of those cattle they worked over, and then I'll spell you on the drill rig."

"You can drill?"

"I have."

At sunup, he and Rex finished the breakfast of the Chinaman, who grumbled the whole time. "Me soonee runnee outee food."

"Don't worry, Dan's going after some," Slocum said to him between bites.

"He don't go soon, all me have is rocks to cook."

Slocum agreed. "He's leaving this morning."

"Hell, I'd like some rock stew," Smoothers said, and laughed.

The Chinaman waved a spoon to threaten him. "I feed you rock stew."

Seated on their butts in leg irons, the prisoners appeared a little grubbier than when they'd surrendered. Slocum looked them over, and he never missed the hard look that Phelps gave him.

"They've been digging a new ditch from the drill site to the tank," Smoothers said. "They needed something to do. Might as well get ready for prison work, huh?"

Slocum grinned and agreed.

"How're we paying for these supplies?" Smoothers asked him under his breath.

"How much do we need?"

"Fifty bucks should do it."

Slocum dug it out and counted it out to Smoothers. "That be enough?"

"I can make up the rest," Smoothers said, and headed over to give it to Dan, who was hitching the team.

Slocum and Rex rode out shortly after Dan left. Haney's drill was pounding the ground when Slocum stepped in the saddle. They rode west, and in a short while spooked some cattle. Uncertain about roping on the big horse, Slocum drove a two-year-old out of the brush, and in two jumps the bay was on his heels. The toss was easy, and Slocum dallied off when he turned the bay sideways. Rex rode in and snared the hocks. When the steer was stretched and down, Slocum ran over and tied three legs on the bawling animal.

Rex examined the brand, holding his hat and scratching his hair. "I can see the run-over marking from here. Them two will see some hot times in Yuma."

"Not in this county."

"They will when I get through. Special judge. Special prosecutor. What else?"

"How we holding them in the sheriff's jail?"

"Gantry'll either hold them or be in contempt."

"But they implicated Worthington."

"Good, he can stand trial, too."

"It gets more complicated. They say Gantry is Worthington's man anyway."

"Things are going to be interesting, ain't they?"

They took the lariats off the steer's head and heels. Slocum undid the tie-down rope and slapped the animal with it on the rump as he got up.

They started back to camp with Slocum promising to show Rex many more altered brands.

"No need. I saw what they're doing. Come roundup time this fall, I'll have three of my toughest men right here to inspect every one in question."

"Can't ask for more than that." Slocum reached out and shook the man's hand.

"A trip to town, and I'll wire the governor and tell him what I found here."

"I'd be concerned that they might have the telegraph man in their pocket," Slocum said.

"I hadn't thought of that."

"Bob mailed the letter out of Barlowville since she was worried about collusion."

Rex nodded. "You might be right. I can handle it. I'm going back up there."

"Good. Maybe Bob and them did some good." Slocum frowned as he rode into camp. Something looked out of place.

"Where are the prisoners?" Rex asked, looking around.

"Let's ride over to the drill rig. Maybe we can find them."

A nauseating pain struck Slocum in the gut—like a mule'd kicked him in the belly. Something was bad wrong. He sure hoped the others were all right. He booted the big horse through camp.

Chapter 12

Smoothers had been shot. The Chinese man was so upset between crying and rushing around frantically, Slocum could hardly get the story out of him. The three prisoners had made a break for it and gotten a gun. Haney and Zeke had gone after them. That worried Slocum more than anything else—those two were certainly not manhunters, and might become cannon fodder.

Smoothers was in some pain. But his shoulder wound looked superficial. He was reclining on a bedroll beside the drill rig. "Damn, I guess you were right. Phelps was planning all the time how to get the jump on us."

"We need the slug out of you," Slocum said, concerned about the man's wound.

"Get it out."

"I'm more butcher than doctor."

"I trust you."

"I'll help," Rex said.

"I'll get it out, but I want that Chinaman to take you over to a woman's place by the Harte ranch. Her name is Marie Goddard and she owns a store."

"What in the hell for?"

"She can get you back on your feet."

"What the hell for? Lo can get me back on my feet."

"Quit arguing, you're going. Now raise up and I'll get that shirt off you."

"I still don't—"

"You will. Trust me, Smoothers, you will. Lo, find him some whiskey. He'll need it."

"What can I do?" Rex asked.

"I'll need some clean bandages. Maybe ride down to the house and find something we can use."

Rex nodded and was gone in a shot.

"Phelps jumped Zeke," Smoothers said. His face was wet with beads of sweat and the pain was evident in his eyes. "And caught him off guard. Zeke had an old .30-caliber black-powder, and Phelps shot me with it. If he'd used the .44/40, I wouldn't be here. He must have had the keys all the time 'cause he unlocked all of the cuffs and they headed out. Dan was already gone for supplies and Haney was busy drilling."

Lo was back with the whiskey and blabbering like a wild man. "No let him die. You fix him, huh? You mend him."

"I'll try."

"No. No. You fix him good."

Slocum wanted a sock to stuff down Lo's throat to shut him up. Satisfied to see Smoothers swigging whiskey out of the bottle, he opened his jackknife and squatted by the fire. Rex shouldn't be too long getting back with something for bandages. He wanted it on hand when he went in after the bullet. He glanced at the faraway hills—Phelps and the others had run north. Maybe Phelps figured his time in the county was over.

"Lo!" Smoothers shouted at the Celestial. "Go wash the dishes and shut up."

Slocum nodded in agreement. Haney and Zeke would be no match for those three, especially Phelps. When Slocum got through doctoring Smoothers, he better go check on Haney and Zeke—things were sure getting into a real mess.

Where was Roberta and Harte? A million things were going on. Gantry might show up next unless he got word about Phelps. Working the jackknife blade over a whetstone, he heard more than one horse coming. He rose and could see three riders. One was Rex, so the other two—Roberta was with him. Good.

He smiled at the sight of her piling off the horse and running to his outstretched arms.

Out of breath, she stopped and frowned at Smoothers, sitting up and drinking whiskey. "What happened to him?"

"He'll be better when I dig the bullet out. How are you?" He hugged her tight.

"Fine. Fine. Oh, that's U.S. Marshal Hodge Williams. The governor sent him."

"Deputy U.S. marshal," the man corrected her. "What happened here?"

"We were holding two rustlers and a deputy sheriff who attacked the drill rig," said Slocum. "They broke out of here and ran earlier today. Two of our men, Haney and a helper named Zeke, went after them."

"Haney went after them?" she asked in disbelief.

"He was already gone when I got here. Rex, did you—"

"Before she got there, I tore up a clean sheet, okay?" He showed him the stack of bandages.

"Sure, fine. I'll heat this knife on the fire and then we can try to extract the bullet. Hey, save some of that whiskey to disinfect the wound," he said to Smoothers.

"Lo! Go get another bottle!" Smoothers shook his head from side to side.

"Rex, you and the marshal hold him down."

"What can I do?" Bob asked.

"Is there some black powder around?"

"Flask in my things—" Smoothers said, lying on his back and shading his eyes from the bright sun with his good arm.

"I'll get it." She scrambled for it.

"Hold him down, boys. I need something for him to bite on so he don't hurt himself."

"There's a leather strap." She waved it, bringing it and the flask over.

When Rex and Williams were ready, Slocum felt with the knife tip in the wound for the bullet. He struck it quickly. It wasn't buried, but without a forceps, he'd have to dislodge it out of the muscle. That meant cutting some of it until he could pry the slug out. He began to gouge, and Smoothers bit down on the strap stuck in his mouth.

Slocum'd seen a bullet-extract screw used in such an operation, but didn't have one now. At least he had the knifepoint to pry with. But the bullet was still lodged.

He went for a new point to pry from, and this time the bullet gave some and Smoothers cried out behind the strap. Then, with all his might, hoping the jackknife blade didn't give or break, Slocum forced the bullet up and out. In his bloody fingers, he showed it to Smoothers.

"We got her."

Smoothers nodded and closed his eyes.

"Bob, while I'm applying the powder to this wound, get a match ready. You think you can start it?"

On her knees beside him, she swallowed hard. "I think so."

"Once you light it, close your eyes, it'll flash." He looked at the other two men holding Smoothers's arms, and they acknowledged his warning.

He began to pour the flakes of black powder on the bloody wound the size of his thumbnail. With his knife blade to push them in, he filled the wound. Then he reared back and nodded. The other two looked away, and she struck the match.

The flash made a whooshing sound and Smoothers wiggled in pain; then he fainted. Slocum nodded. "We need to bandage that shoulder. That should sear the bleeding off and disinfect it."

Pale-faced, she rose. "Tough treatment, I'd say."

"If we saved his life, he won't complain."

"But what if we didn't?"

"Then he won't complain either."

She shook her head in disapproval; the other two laughed. Slocum bandaged Smoothers and tied the cloth off.

"What now?" she asked.

"Someone needs to stay with him. Then we can go find those three."

"The cook can watch him," Rex said, indicating Lo.

"I guess. We'll need to be back here later." Slocum looked around, and at last spotted the cook. "Lo, you watch after him."

"Me watch bossy. Him no die?"

"No, he'll be fine. Make him comfortable. I'll check on Dan, too," he said to the barely coherent Smoothers.

The man nodded. Bob had gone and brought back Slocum's horse.

"When I saw Baldy in the corral at the Harte ranch, I about died," she said to him, handing over the reins. "I thought you must be dead."

"His man Nevada loaned me this big devil. What's Harte doing?"

"He and another marshal went after Gantry. There is a special judge coming to hold a grand jury investigation, and Searles should be released in ten days."

"Good news."

"So much has been happening and I worried so much about you. No way to get you word, so we rode over to see."

"Haney is down a hundred feet with the well. He and Zeke had no business going after those killers, but they went before I got back here. Rex's seen the brands they blotched. So he'll have some inspectors here at roundup time."

"I know, he told me already," she said.

In the saddle, they joined the others and rode north. Slocum took the lead on the big bay. The tracks were fresh enough, and soon they were in the juniper country. There was no sighting of Haney and Zeke besides their tracks, but they were ahead somewhere.

She rode side by side with him. "What I saw of him, Haney sure didn't look to me like a posse man."

"He may surprise you."

She smiled over at him. "I will be surprised if he does anything besides get himself hurt."

Slocum saw the dust on the horizon and a wagon coming. "That may be Dan. Perhaps he knows something."

"There are riders and horses, too," she pointed out.

Dan reined the team in, and Haney rode up and took off his hat for her. "Howdy, Miss Bakker, sure glad to see you again. We've got Dawson and Manley, but Phelps got away."

Slocum nodded, seeing the look of surprise on her face.

"How did you do it?" she asked as they began to dismount.

"We found them making camp and me and Zeke snuck up on them. Phelps had already gone somewhere when we got the drop on them."

"Where had he gone?" Slocum asked.

"We think Barlowville. But we figured we had two of them, so we started back and met Dan."

"Anyone of you have any idea where he is now? I mean Phelps." Slocum looked over at the three men. When they shook their heads, he went over to the wagon and looked at the two bound prisoners.

"Where did Phelps go?"

"To town, I guess. He said there was an Indian had a gold mine. He planned to track him down and then come back for us," Dawson said.

"Joe Black Horse?" Slocum asked.

"Yeah," Manley grunted. "That was who it was. Said we'd all be rich."

"I bet." Slocum shook his head. "You boys would have grown whiskers there waiting for Phelps to come back."

"What now?" Williams asked.

"You better take them two back to Antelope Springs," he said to Williams and Rex. "Haney has a well to drill. I'll go see if I can find Phelps. He's got a way of being elusive. If we all go up there, he'll get spooked and run."

When he turned to Bob, she was looking at her dusty boots. "Guess I'll go along and hold the horses."

Slocum nodded and shook hands with Haney and Zeke, congratulating them for their good work. "We'll be back in a few days if we can't turn up anything."

Dan climbed on the wagon and nodded to him. They were off, leaving Bob and Slocum in the dusty ruts watching them pull away.

"What now?" she asked him.

"We'll go to Barlowville and try to learn where Joe Black Horse is at. He may lead us to Phelps."

"But I thought Phelps was going to follow Joe."

"Joe's the bait."

"I see."

Slocum bounded up onto the saddle and checked the big horse. She swung a chap-clad leg over the saddle and settled in place. "Let's go. I want that sumbitch."

"So do I, girl. So do I."

Chapter 13

A bloody sunset drenched the western sky. Wrapped in the head-high greasewood, Barlowville was about to be swallowed in darkness. Already, long shadows cast by the mountains spread over the sprawling jacales and tin-roofed businesses. Slocum and Bob rode slowly up the gravel ruts. Be a damn good place for an ambush.

They found a handwritten note on Rip's store and post office, which was shuttered and barred. *Gone to collect a bad debt.* Slocum reined his horse around, disappointed. Rip might have known where Joe was at. They rode on up the dirt street.

On the right, he nodded toward a crude sign that said CAFE. They dismounted to hitch their horses at the rack. No other horses were around and he could not see anything out of place, but the unusual tall growth of the stiff brush made for poor vision. There were few places where the creosote-smelling brush grew this high. He remembered seeing such a growth east of the Superstitions where he'd evaded an Apache war party in the greasewood.

"You know this place?" she asked in a whisper.

He shook his head. "It don't suit, we'll go elsewhere."

Lights were on inside and they walked into the room.

127

"Ah, Señor and Señorita, so nice to have you," a smiling, ample-bodied woman said with a slight bow.

"Thank you," Slocum said. "What's for supper?"

"*Cabrito*. Slow-cooked and very tender."

He exchanged a questioning look with Bob, who nodded her approval. "Goat sounds good, and some wine."

"The wine is red," the woman warned, showing them the table.

"Is there any other color?" he asked. They both laughed.

An old man came from the back, sat in a chair, and played the guitar while they ate. They were the songs of Mexico—the wild horse, the love gone wrong, the woman who left him. Some miners floured in gray dust came in and stole glances at Bob. They, too, laughed along with the woman.

She kept the wineglasses full and fluttered over Slocum and Bob. Then one of the miners shouted at the musician to go get his trumpet. He rose and carefully set aside the ancient guitar. Back bent, he waved at their teasing and went to find the horn.

He returned, and Slocum wondered how so frail-looking a person could even raise a note on the battered brass instrument in his gnarled hands. But raise he did, with the haunting "No Quarter" that Santa Anna played at the Alamo before attacking. His notes even silenced the miners. When he finished, he took a bow and they all applauded him.

Then he played a polka, and one of the miners danced with the woman, sweeping her around the tables to the hand clapping and shouts of the other men.

"I'm glad we found this place," Bob said.

Slocum nodded.

When the old man stopped playing, Slocum leaned over and asked the table of miners if they had seen Joe Black Horse that day. They shook their heads.

"I saw him last night," one of the men said. "Why?"

"There is a man who bragged he was going to find Joe's mine who came up here today. He's a killer."

"What's he look like?" one of them asked.

Slocum turned to Bob to describe him.

"He's in his thirties, has dark curly hair that's long, and he looks like a dandy all the time."

"I saw him at the mercantile earlier," one of the men said. "Wasn't he a deputy?"

"Yes," Slocum said. "One of Gantry's men."

"Is he here to kill Joe?"

Slocum shrugged. "We don't know. We just heard he was coming up here to steal Joe's mine."

"Let us know if you need any help. We'll sure cave in his head if he messes with that old Injun."

"Yeah, Joe's the only guy ever buys us free drinks."

Slocum paid the woman, tipped the old man, and thanked the miners. Outside in the starlight, they walked to their horses.

"What now?" she asked.

"Check the saloons."

"How many are there?"

"Two or three."

She hugged her arms and looked about in the darkness. "He could be anywhere around here?"

"He sure could. The game is cat and mouse."

"What're we?"

"The cat, I hope." He reached out and hugged her shoulders before they mounted up. "I don't think he knows we're here—yet."

"Where will we stay tonight?"

On his horse, he slapped the bedroll tied on behind. "Here."

She laughed. "One thing to look forward to anyway."

The first saloon he went in to check was full of Mexicans. The black-mustached bartender had not seen this gringo that Slocum described and Old Joe had not been in there all day. Slocum thanked him and gave him two bits.

The second saloon was the Red Horse. The smoke inside

was thicker than in the first one. More dust-coated miners with haggard looks written on their faces eyed him suspiciously.

The bartender told him the man he wanted had been in there earlier, but Old Joe had not been in all day. He had not seen Phelps since then either. Slocum tipped him, thanked him, and headed through the smoke for the door.

"I know where that guy you're looking for is at," a miner behind him said.

Slocum turned, and the short man following him carried a mug of sudsy brew in his hand. "You do?"

"Worth a few beers?"

"Sure." Slocum dug in his vest for two quarters and slapped them on the bar. "Where is he?"

"Up at Soapy Jones's place."

"Where's that?"

"Mile up the road, you can't miss it. Soapy keeps some *putas* and there's some no-accounts hang around up there."

"Mister—" another miner, well in his cups, put in. "It's a good place to get your ass robbed." Then, nodding his head like a loose cannon, he stepped back to his beer at the bar.

"Either of you seen Old Joe today?" Slocum asked.

"No, why?"

"This guy Phelps bragged he'd get Old Joe's mine."

Both of them laughed at the notion. "Been better men have tried," the sober one said.

Slocum thanked them and went out to his horse handler.

"Learn anything?" she asked.

"They said Phelps is or was at Soapy's."

"Soapy Jones's house of ill repute?"

"I guess you know about it?"

She smiled. "Only what I overheard growing up as a girl in this country."

"Must be a tough place. One old drunk in there said they robbed folks."

"It has a bad reputation, but it's the only whorehouse for

miles. So I think when men can't stand it anymore, they take their chances and go there."

"And get robbed."

"Well—they usually don't take more money than they need." She swung on her horse.

"We better ride up and see if he's there."

"Sure. I can hold the horses."

Slocum chuckled. He really was thinking about a night out in the brush with her silky flesh to knead and pound. But his own pleasures had to wait until after he'd checked out all the places where Phelps might be hiding.

There were a few horses hitched outside Soapy's. Slocum looked them over trying to see if he recognized any of them. A player piano was going on inside, and the sounds of women's laughter carried into the night. An occasional male outburst would join them, followed by more put-on laughing. It was all part of the stupid games they played in such dens of sin. "Oh, why are you here tonight?" and "Oh, I never do that."

Bob shook her head when they finished looking at the horses. "I don't know any of these horses," she said.

"Me either. Sometimes in a bear's den you flush out a bear. Be on your guard."

"You be careful." She slapped the .30-caliber on her hip. "I can use it."

He kissed her on the forehead and headed for the brightly lit front doorway of the rambling adobe house. He checked the Colt and then reset the holster. No telling what he'd find beyond the threshold.

For long moment, he stood a few feet from the doorway to let his eyes adjust to the brighter light inside. A blond woman in a billowing nightshirt appeared in the doorway and smiled, showing her missing tooth.

"Come on in here. I thought I heard someone ride up."

He nodded and stepped inside the room. Several hard looks were cast his direction from a card game under a wagon-wheel candle lamp. But no one seemed jarred by his appearance and the men turned back to the game.

"Well?" the woman asked, attached to his left arm. "Poker or poke me?"

Then she threw back her head and laughed. "Get it? Poker or poke me?"

He nodded. She must've taken a bath in cheap perfume. She reeked of it and her body had a musky smell. Her last bath had not been recent—her hair was oily despite the gold color plastered on her head. She had large boobs that she shoved into his arm, and an obvious potbelly that she pressed to his side as she guided him toward a bar.

"Well, darling, who we got here?" the bartender, a gray-whiskered man, asked, setting a bottle of bonded whiskey on the bar.

"Here's a bottle of good whiskey. That and her ass'll cost you three bucks," the man said. "Want to stay all night and try to wear the hole out, it'll cost you four bucks." The man's blue eyes were as hard as the words that he spoke. He had to be Soapy.

"What if I don't like it?"

"Her or the whiskey?"

"Either."

"I don't give no gawdamn refunds."

"I just asked. Pour me a shot. I'll try it."

Soapy never took his eyes off him and slapped a jigger on the bar. "You're new around here."

"First time."

She laughed and rubbed her belly against him. "It's good stuff."

"I never doubted it." Slocum poured a shot from the bottle. "I'm looking for a deputy sheriff from Saguaro County named Phelps."

"This ain't—"

"Saguaro County. I know that. He ain't a deputy there

no more." He tossed down the drink and nodded in approval. It was smooth whiskey.

"We going upstairs now?" she whined.

"You seen him today?" he asked Soapy, ignoring her.

"Maybe."

Slocum pushed her hand away from taking the whiskey. "He still here?"

"Who should I tell him was calling?"

"I can tell him that myself."

Soapy considered the bottle, then Slocum. "You the law?"

"No, if I had been, I'd already have showed you a badge."

"Guess this is private? I mean between you and him."

"You could call it that. What room's he in?"

"Down the hall, third one on the left. What's your name?"

"Slocum."

"I'll put it on your tombstone."

Slocum laid three dollars on the bar. "I'll be back for the whiskey."

"What about me?" the woman whined.

"Your money's there."

He started for the hall and heard Soapy say, "Don't shoot the whore. They ain't easy to get."

He didn't bother to answer him. The hallway was dark. It smelled of sweat and the sour unmistakable musk of women involved in selling their bodies. The third door was locked when he tried it with his left hand.

The player piano had stopped. A pin could have dropped. Gun in his right fist, he used his boot to smash open the door. The flash of a gun's orange muzzle blast answered him, and the room boiled in gun smoke and adobe dust from the shot in the wall. A woman inside gave a shrill scream that cut the night. He knew someone was getting away out a window, but there was nothing he dared do.

He holstered the Colt and rushed for the front door—the horses. Out in front, he met Bob. "Did he come this way?"

She looked relieved to see he was unscathed. "No, he must have had his horse in back. I heard him ride off."

"Damn. I have to go back in and get my whiskey."

"Sure," she said, and went back to their horses.

He crossed to the bar, the gamblers under the smoky yellow light glancing at him again. He shook his head at the blond whore and, looking disappointed, she moved away.

Slocum took the bottle and looked Soapy in the eye. "Next time you signal some bastard that I'm after, I'll skin your hide and nail it on the shithouse door."

"Signal? Huh?"

Slocum gave him a smug smile and gestured with the hand with the bottle. "That damn piano stopped playing. Now it's started up again."

"If you ain't the law, who in the fuck are you?"

"A mad sumbitch who for two cents would pistol-whip you within an inch of your life." He turned on his heel before he did it and headed for the door.

"Slocum? Slocum?"

He stopped in the door, not turning. "Yes?"

"He said you'd be coming."

"Good, now he knows I did."

He had Phelps on the move and as far as he knew, the ex-deputy hadn't found Joe Black Horse—so far.

"Where are we going?" Bob asked when he joined her.

"To find a bed." He swung a leg over his horse.

"Now we're getting to the good stuff."

He sat in the saddle. *Wherever you are, Phelps, I'll find your ass.* Meanwhile, he'd enjoy some of the pleasures in life—her body. Thinking for a second about the smelly, snaggle-toothed blond whore back there made a shudder run through his body.

Chapter 14

A cool predawn wind swept his cheek. How the heat of the day before could evaporate so much overnight, he'd never know. His hand gently fondled her firm teardrop breast as she nestled against him. She groaned in pleasure and reached back to rub her palm on his bare hip.

"What do we do today?" she asked in a sleep-husky voice.

"Go look for Joe Black Horse. He's our bait."

"Where will he be? No one has ever seen his mine."

"No, but they know what direction it must be in."

"How will we find out?" She wiggled against him.

"Rip should be back from his debt collecting. He's Joe's man."

She rolled over to face him and reached down to pull on his dick. "Are we in a hurry?"

He closed his eyes and yawned. "Suit yourself."

"I mean, are we?" Her hand action was already making him think about it.

"I guess not."

"Good." She kissed him, then with a mischievous look on her face, climbed on top of his legs to pump him harder with her fist. His tool was responding fast.

The cool air began to seek his skin, but in minutes she was riding his pole and he didn't give a damn. Oh, his balls would ache when this was over. He closed his eyes and savored her intense presence bouncing on top of him.

When they rode into town, he found a woman selling bean burritos at the edge of the road. He ordered two, paid her, gave one to his partner, and then they rode on busy eating breakfast. The U.S. flag flapped over Rip's store when they dismounted, and the door was open signaling his return.

They went inside and Rip looked up at Bob. "That dang governor never sent you a letter here anyway."

"Oh, he answered me all right. I went to see him, too, and he sent lots of help."

"I'd never believed he'd've done a damn thing. What can I do for you today?"

"There's a former deputy from Antelope Springs made some big talk to some other outlaws that he was coming over here and finding Joe Black Horse's mine."

"I wish him luck."

"No, Rip, he's liable to kill Joe," Slocum said. "The man's cold-blooded enough to be big trouble for Joe." Bob reinforced Slocum's words with a sharp nod.

"Joe may be an old drunk, but he's still an Apache."

"Give us the general area of the mine and we'll go see if we can stop him."

"Why? What's that old buck done for you two?"

"We want to take Phelps back and face trial for other crimes."

"What did he do?" Rip looked from him to her.

She stepped forward and used her finger to point at her chest. "He raped me twice."

"Oh, Lord, dear me. I'm sorry. That mine is up near Peralta Canyon. Sorry, he never told me any more than that."

"Can you draw us a map to get there?" Slocum asked

"Sure."

Rip put butcher paper on top of the counter, and used a pencil to sketch out the area and the route they'd need to take to get there.

"There's a spring up there near the top of this trail. Folks said the Spaniards used this trail to pack the gold out on. They must have used this spring, too. It's a sure one. But as to where to go when you get up there, I don't know."

"Thanks. We'll try to stop Phelps from hurting Joe."

"You two be careful up there. They say some renegades still use that trail going back and forth to Mexico from San Carlos."

"Sure, we'll be damn careful," Slocum agreed. "We'll need some jerky and a mix of cornmeal and brown sugar to take with us. Way I figure it, the next few days we'll be feasting out a lot up there." He winked at her.

Rip laughed and went to fetch their needs. They rode out of the community and headed for the hills that fringed the north end of the basin. At mid-morning, they reached an abandoned shack with a spring-fed tank. The day had warmed and she asked if they had time for a bath.

"That water sure looks inviting."

He agreed, and since they were halfway to Peralta Canyon, he began toeing off his boots. "Let's do it. May be our last chance for a while."

The waist-deep tank was mossy, but the water was sun-warmed and he knew that it would be a good place to bathe. She quickly undressed and in minutes was swimming across the walled tank, her white skin shining in the brilliant sun that danced on the surface. He left his gun and belt on the wall and climbed in.

She waded over and hugged him. "What will I do when you are gone?"

He rocked her back and forth. "You're a survivor. You'll make it."

She threw her head back and looked up at him. "How soon will you have to go?"

He shook her playfully and grimaced. "Those Kansas deputies that Gantry sent for will be here soon."

She buried her face in his chest. "I know. I know."

"When I'm gone, I want you to think real hard about Haney."

"Haney?" She looked pained at him.

"He's real and he is fascinated with you."

"Fascinated? I mean, he's such a dude."

"Him and Zeke caught those other two."

"They must have just given up."

"No, he planned it and it took nerve. He'd fight dragoons for you."

She frowned in disbelief at him.

Slocum ignored her look. "We better get dry and on the trail."

"Yes, bossy."

Dressed again and in the saddle, they rode on north. By mid-afternoon, Slocum was satisfied the trail that entered the canyon was the one they needed to take. He checked for any prints and found nothing new, which he hoped meant that Phelps was not up there waiting for Joe or for him and her.

The sheer brown, red, and gray walls quickly began to swallow them. The click of their horses' shoes echoed in the deepening canyon. In places, the pathway was crushed gravel. In other spots, the trail went over exposed rock outcroppings worn some over the years by travelers. It first climbed skyward through the chaparral; then live oaks began to drape overhead. Soon, a few junipers and piñons spiked the crowded vegetation in the dense foliage on the floor of the canyon.

"I hear water," she said.

He nodded. Except for the many birds chirping and singing, the canyon had been silent. Now, a trickle of water could be heard off to their right in the dense brush in the wash area. Soon, they came to a flat and above them, a small stream of water spilled off a red rock ledge, falling some ten feet into a bathtublike pool in the rock formation.

"Oh, my, isn't that wonderful."

"Yes, in the middle of this godforsaken country, it looks like heaven." He dropped from the saddle and let his sea legs recover a moment before turning loose of the horn. The towering heights on both sides still soared above them, like the lone vulture gliding overhead.

"What do we do next?" she asked.

"Stow these horses. I think there is a side canyon over there, if we can get to it."

"Want me to go look?"

"No, I'll go and see."

She agreed, and began undoing the cinches. With a wave to send him on, she fought the latigos loose. He climbed over some house-sized rocks, and soon found that getting into the side canyon would have to be on foot. Then he jumped down into the wash area and saw something shining in the sand.

He dropped down and recovered it. It was hexagon-shaped with a hole in the center. At first, he began to polish it on his pants, and immediately saw it was a gold coin with Spanish words on it.

"Bob. Bob, come here." His heart stopped as he searched around the dizzy heights. She soon appeared, and he pocketed the find to catch her when she jumped off the rock into his arms. Then he set her down.

"What is it?"

"Wait till you see what I found." He dug out the ancient coin.

"My, oh, my, it's gold, isn't it?"

He nodded quickly. "It was here in the sand when I jumped down. There may be more." He swallowed hard. "I don't know how old it is, but it's old. They've been making round ones for years."

"Is there more here?" She searched around the area.

"This one was in the sand partly exposed, probably by the last rainstorm."

She nodded and began shifting the silty dirt through her fingers. In a moment, she gave a cry. "I've got another. No, two more."

He looked around to check things, then paused, filled with a new fear. This gold fever could get so bad they'd lose all their sense, and someone would discover the horses and then get the drop on them.

"Yes, yes, fine, but we need to take our horses out of this canyon. We're easy targets—"

"There's more here," she cried, holding up handfuls of the coins with sand sifting out of them.

"We have to move the horses and now," he declared.

She scrambled to her feet, slapping dirt off her hands and chaps. She joined him, out of breath. "We're rich, Slocum. We're rich."

Her arms encircled his waist and she squeezed him tight. "Hear me, we're rich. Those are old Spanish gold doubloons."

"I know. I know. But we need to move the horses. Hide our tracks. Phelps isn't a damn fool, and neither is that old drunk Indian Joe."

Her face flushed with excitement, she gulped for air. "All right. All right. What do we need to do first?"

"Take the horses over this pass above us to where there is water and grass for them."

She nodded. "Let's go. How did these doubloons get here?"

He tightened his girth. "Maybe conquistadors. Indians wanted to return all the gold back to the earth where it came from. They could have ditched it there. The Spaniards could have dropped a sackful off in haste and not returned or known how to get back."

"Is it part of Joe's mine?"

He shook his head. "I'd say it might have been part of

the Spanish operation. This's been mined, refined, and poured into a stamp mill."

"Why would they do that?"

"Taxes." He swung on his horse. "If they'd returned to Mexico with enriched gold ore, then the officials would have taxed them for all of it. But money, they'd've never known its source."

"How do you know that?"

"The reverse happened to a mine I ran in Mexico. I could bring ore out of there and not pay a twenty-percent tariff if I had the ore processed at a U.S. refinery. So I put the bars in the bottom of the panniers and covered them in high-grade ore. At the border, the customs man looked briefly at a few panniers and let us in."

He sent the bay up the steep trail and said over his shoulder, "The man at the refinery asked why I even bothered to bring so little ore out of Mexico for him to refine, but I didn't tell him."

Her horse on his heels, she laughed. Excitement was boiling out of her. "Can we get it out?"

"We need to be careful. Word ever gets out about what we've found—there'll be a gold rush up here."

"Oh, I thought we only had to worry about Phelps and maybe Joe."

He twisted in the saddle and looked back past her for any sight of company. Nothing but the dense live oak and junipers, with a few century-plant stolons sticking up, to make a thick curtain.

At last, they emerged on top of the pass. A strong cool wind swept his face, and he could look out over lots of mesas and broken ranges. There were some green cottonwood clusters far below, which meant they should find water and forage down there.

He stepped off the bay as she joined him. "We can stow my bedroll and our saddlebags up here. Save us packing them back up here when we come out of there on foot."

She nodded her approval and turned to undo her bags.

In no time, the roll and bags were hidden under some juniper bows and he had taken the bay by the reins to lead him off the steep trail. She also came on foot leading her pony. The top of the trail was straight down with loose gravel for a hundred feet. Then it began a crisscross pattern. The bay horse slipped in a narrow ditch, and almost pulled Slocum downhill with him.

With nothing to hang on to, he did some fancy footwork and shouted for Bob to let her horse go. They'd catch it at the bottom. He did the same with the bay. Three lengths down the mountain, the gelding was on his knees scrambling, but found his footing and still looked sound going on down, followed by her pony, who skidded with the skill of a mountain horse.

He caught her by the waist when she came sliding on her soles past him waving her arms for balance. They both went down with a laugh. He looked in her face and smiled.

"Be a shame after finding all that gold to get killed falling down a mountain."

She threw her arms around his neck and kissed him. "Mmm, it would be."

When they separated, he sat up on his butt, legs outstretched, and shook his head, looking down the slope to where the two horses stood waiting on the first flat. "We better move on."

"Are we going to wait for Phelps?"

"Yes, for a day. Then if he don't show, we can go back with your gold."

"It's partially yours," she said, looking hurt.

He shook his head. "I don't need that much money. It'll make your operation a success with or without an artesian well."

"I can't—"

He put his finger on her mouth to silence her. "I know. You will be much better off and I want that. Now let's get down there and hobble the horses so we can climb out and watch for Phelps." He found it strange that the deputy had not shown up in the area by now.

Slocum found some live water in the wash that would be accessible for a hobbled horse. There was plenty of grama grass and side oats graze for the horses. When they were chomping grass, he looked at the mountain, ready to go back up.

She grimaced and then smiled. "Looks twice as long as it did coming down."

"Ah, just a hike. I'll push."

"I may need it," she said, and started up the trail.

After a few minutes, they paused to catch their breath and looked back over the broken country.

"Lots of places to hide a mine out there," she said.

He agreed. Probably why Joe had kept his own mine a secret.

"I'm ready," she announced.

He looked toward the pass. Where was Phelps? He might have taken a powder and run. With a sigh, Slocum started up one step at a time, looking past her toward the pass. It would be good to be up there.

On top, they sat on a large rock and rested. The day was fading fast, and the notion of chewing on peppery jerky didn't appeal to him. It was good that he had her for company.

"We better go find our things before it gets dark."

She agreed, looking weary. When she stood, he kissed her and hugged her tight. "This will all be over soon," he promised her.

Chapter 15

"Don't make a move." Phelps stepped out from behind the house-sized rock with a gun in his hand. "Well, if it ain't Slocum and Bob."

The only other sound Slocum heard was the spill of water over the small falls. His heart sunk. How had he walked into such a trap? All Phelps had to do was sit and wait for them to return. Damn. If he'd been by himself he'd've taken him on, but he couldn't risk Bob being in the middle of a shoot-out.

"Stand there," Phelps said, and slipped around, taking her gun first. Then, with it in his waistband, he slipped behind Slocum.

Time to take action. Slocum drove his elbow backward and threw Phelps off balance. Then he whirled and caught the barrel of Phelps's six-gun and drove it skyward. The muzzle blast was deafening in the canyon. The bullet went skyward. Acrid gun smoke filled the air and burned Slocum's eyes.

He drove his fist into Phelps's midsection, and the outlaw gasped for breath. Then he ripped the Colt from Phelps's grasp, and the outlaw froze at the sight of a .44/40.

"Give me an excuse to blow you to hell and gone," Bob said through her teeth, holding the rifle on Phelps.

Phelps collapsed. "I should have killed you seven years ago," he said to Slocum.

"Think about it. You've had seven more years to live than if you'd tried it back in Kansas."

"Go to hell."

"I can count that you'll be there ahead of me." Slocum took a big knife off Phelps. "Where's your cuffs?"

"I lost 'em."

"Good, I've got rope. You can't unlock it." Slocum nodded to Bob in the twilight. "Well, now we can go back and get the horses."

"Oh, damn. What a waste."

"It turned out all right."

"I guess. We'd've never found the gold if we hadn't come."

"You found the mine?" Phelps asked, blinking at them.

"No, just traces of folks being here," Slocum replied.

"I followed that damn Injun in here and lost him. His mine is around here somewhere."

With some rope from his saddlebags, Slocum made sure that his prisoner's hands were tied tight behind his back. Then he tied his feet and set him on the ground. "Try something and I won't waste any lead on wounding you."

"I still should have killed you."

"We all have things that we regret in our lives." He turned to Bob. "Supper will be jerky."

"Fine. What about him?"

"I'm not worried about him."

"Neither am I. What's the plan?"

"Get all the doubloons we can find. I'll go get the horses first thing in the morning and we'll ride back with him."

"He have a horse?" she asked.

"He don't have one, he can walk."

"I've got one stashed down the canyon," Phelps said.

"Good, you won't have to walk all the way."

They chewed on their jerky, then Slocum made a small

fire for light. On their hands and knees, they crawled over the alluvial sand and combed out the coins.

"How long have these been here, do you reckon?" she asked as the pile grew.

"Not long."

"What do you mean?" She looked up from her search under the starlight.

He tossed another coin over to clink on the pile. "If they'd been here long, some prospector going by and panning for gold would have found them."

"How did they get here?"

"This rotten sack broke and spilled them." He held up the old leather purse he'd found in the dirt.

Raising up on her knees, she shook her head. "Why didn't they pick them up?"

"They probably had enough and didn't want to lose any time getting out of here."

"Who would these people be?"

"We'll probably never know."

"Nice of them to leave it anyway."

In a few hours, they decided the thirty-four coins in the pile were all they'd find. Wearily, they loaded the saddlebags with their loot.

"It's been a long day," he said, shouldering the heavy bags. Then he reached down to pull her to her feet.

"A real long one," she agreed.

At the spring, he checked Phelps's ropes and figured he'd stay hitched. Then they went up the path and he spread out his bedroll on a small patch of dry grass. She sat down on it and he pulled off her boots, then toed off his own as she peeled down her chaps.

She rose free of them and shed her canvas pants. The glow of her shapely legs in the starlight made him smile. In a short while, she stood naked in the pearly night. Arms folded over her pear-shaped breasts, she shuddered.

"It's been a while."

"Too long," he said, pulling off his pants.

"Have we forgot how?"

He swept her to his naked form. "I seriously doubt it."

"Good." She wiggled her warm flesh against him. Then she clutched him tight as the cool night wind swept over them.

In seconds, they were in the bedroll. He inserted his half-full erection in her moist gates, using his grasp on the shaft to stiffen it, and she raised her butt off the bedroll for all of him. It responded, and soon was turgid as he pushed it in and out.

Her mouth open, she tossed her head in pleasure's arms as he ploughed a path into her. Moans of her delirious ecstasy escaped her lips. He speeded up his drives and she clutched his forearms. With his back arched, he drove his dick deep in her and let it fly. They collapsed in a pile and soon fell asleep.

In the predawn, Slocum slipped out, dressed, and went down to check on Phelps. The outlaw, lying on his side, was sawing a log. He looked secure enough. Back at the bedroll, he woke Bob.

"Keep a gun handy and shoot him if he tries anything. I'll be back in a while with our horses."

"I hate—" She sat up and hugged the covers to her chest. "I mean, I can go down there."

"You can catch them if I send them over the top."

"I will." And she pursed her lips for him to kiss.

He did, and then started out. His descent into the shadowy canyon went quickly. When the horses were caught and watered, he saddled them and rode the bay to the steepest area while leading Bob's horse. Then he tied the bay's reins over the saddle horn. Dismounting, he slapped him on the butt and sent him up the grade.

Slocum watched him struggle upward, then fixed the reins on Bob's pony. The bay lost some footing and looked back. Slocum scooped up a rock, threw it, hit him in the butt, and shouted, "Get up there!"

The bay scrambled to the top and Bob grabbed his reins. Then Slocum sent her pony up. He was more of a mountain horse, and put his head down and cat-hopped to the top.

"Got 'em," she called down. Then Slocum climbed up.

At the top, heaving for breath, he bent over, his hands on his knees, and ignored her concern. "Mount up. We need to get back."

She looked worried about him as he swung onto the bay and motioned for her to get mounted. His legs ached from the climb, but he wanted out of this confining canyon with Bob, the gold, and their prisoner. He sent Phelps marching ahead with his hands still tied. With the gold loaded over each saddle, and the temperature rising, they headed downhill.

By midday, they were out of the canyon. Phelps's hands were tied to the saddle horn on his horse, which he was now riding. They hurried across country, arriving at the camp by supper time.

Haney came on the run to meet her. "You want some good news?"

She nodded, dismounting, looking at Slocum for some help.

"Go see," he said, and shooed them off.

His arm in a sling, Smoothers came over and squatted down. "Willams took those two prisoners to town." He looked around before he said anything. "Was I delirious or did I hear you talk about a woman for me?"

"There's a widow woman named Marie Goddard has a crossroads store over by Harte's ranch. I promised I'd introduce you to her."

Smoothers shook his head. "I don't need another woman. Mine's dead."

"So is her husband. They killed him."

"Who else have they killed? Guess it wouldn't hurt for

me to ride over there and introduce myself, since I can't do much around here."

Slocum agreed. "Do that. Marie's a great lady."

Haney and Bob came back from the drill rig.

"The well is a hundred and fifty feet deep," she said. "He's into some hard rock. The kind that usually holds artesian water."

Haney beamed proudly. "It's all guessing, but I think we're close."

Slocum agreed. He made sure that his prisoner was secure and then went to find some food. He left Bob and Haney talking as he went to Lo's cooking outfit under a wind-flapping canvas fly.

Bob and Haney joined him.

"I'm taking Phelps to town," Slocum said after filling his plate with rice and beef.

"I better go along," she said.

"No. My Kansas friends may be there."

"Friends?" She made a frown, then nodded at her own discovery. "You could—ah—be involved, huh?"

"I could."

"Is the bay all right? You could get a ranch horse."

"He's fine. Thanks."

She wet her lips, looked off at the mountains, which were distorted with heat waves, and at last nodded solemnly. "Take some of the coins. You may need them."

"I'll take two."

"Good," she said.

"Haney's going to need new wheels under his rig after he gets your well finished."

"I guess you won't be able to make those spokes?"

"You can afford to fix 'em."

"Sure." She smiled to herself and then nodded.

After he finished the plate and thanked Lo, he fed Phelps some jerky and then loaded him on his horse. Bob was there by the horses when he tightened the cinch.

"You ever need anything, you can call on me," she said. "I owe you some wages beside everything else."

"Naw. We get Worthington and him out of this country." He indicated Phelps. "It'll be a much better place to live. Are they pardoning your brother?"

"The governor promised he'd be a free man and home in two weeks."

"Good."

She used her boot toe to scuff in the dust and spoke under her breath. "You think Haney's the one?"

He rested his arms on the seat of his saddle and nodded. "Why?"

"If he is, I won't pain him by kissing you good-bye."

"Don't pain him." He kissed her cheek and mounted his horse. "Good luck, my amigo."

A smile beamed on her face. "Thanks big man—wait." She dug in the saddlebags over her own kac and handed him two of the coins.

Slocum pocketed them with a nod and rode off leading his prisoner. Haney would make the man she needed. After Slocum got Phelps in jail, he'd be heading out of this country. Maybe he'd get all that done before those two Abbott brothers arrived.

He booted the bay horse on.

Chapter 16

The high-powered shot echoed across the land. The horse under Phelps crumpled and Slocum tossed the lead, bailing off the bay. "Get down! They're out to kill you!"

With his knife, he slashed the ropes on Phelps's hands to free him. Then Slocum dragged him behind the body of his kicking horse so both men were belly-down on the ground.

"That was a buffalo gun," Slocum said.

"I know. I skinned some buff as a kid. That shooter is over a half mile from here." Phelps's face looked pale and his hands quaked. He squeezed them together to attempt to stop the shaking, but that made his body shake.

"Who's got that kind of rifle?" Slocum asked.

Phelps shook his head, recovering some of his composure. "I don't know who—"

"Worthington hire an assassin?"

"Jesus, I ain't talked to him in over a week. How would I know?"

On his elbows and belly behind the horse, Slocum felt grateful it had stopped kicking and died. "It ain't my crew shooting at us," he said.

"I-I ain't certain."

"He was the one calling the shots, wasn't he?"

"You know so much, you figure it out."

Slocum raised up enough and sneaked a peek in the direction he thought the bullet had come from, then ducked back down. There was nothing he could see out there in the scattered junipers and bunchgrass—but he knew the shooter could see *him* through his scope if he wanted to.

"Any reason why he wanted you dead?"

Phelps shrugged and shook his head. He'd sulled up again. Slocum wasn't going to concern himself over that. But it would be dark before they risked going after the bay horse. He had lots better things to do than lie on his belly all day behind a dead horse who, despite his demise, was still farting.

After midnight, Slocum rode up to the jail and made Phelps get down from behind. He hoped the deputy U.S. marshal was in charge of the facility. The man in the doorway was unfamiliar to him.

"U.S. Marshal Williams here?" he asked, wondering if he'd walked into a trap.

"No, sir, he's getting some sleep. Harte and I are watching the jail."

"That you, Slocum?" Harte shouted from inside, and came on the run. "We've been wondering where you were at. Hell, you have Phelps. Come on in here. We've got a bed for you."

Phelps never said anything. He went past Slocum, and Harte hustled him toward the cells as they all entered the lighted room.

"Gantry not in there?" Slocum asked, seeing only the two rustlers in the other cell.

The second man shook his head. "He's been making himself scarce. Someone must have given him the word. He quit the posse and took a powder before we could get down there to arrest him."

"He'll turn up," Harte said, striding back from his lockup.

"Well, today, someone with a high-powered rifle tried to kill Phelps and kept us pinned down all day up there," said Slocum. "They got his horse."

"Who do you figure that would be?" Harte asked, pinching his jaw.

Slocum shook his head. "I wondered, too, who thought he was worth a ten-cent bullet."

"Let's go up and eat at Gloria's. You probably have missed some meals," Harte said.

"She still open this late?"

"Yeah, we can catch her."

At the sight of Slocum coming in the café, Gloria set down a stack of dirty dishes, rushed over, and hugged him. "You're all right after all of this?"

"Fine."

"How's the girl?" She stepped back and put the wave of hair from her face in place.

"Waiting for a gusher. She's fine."

"Good. Guess you haven't ate anything in a month of Sundays. Has he, Jeff?"

"I bet not."

"Well, we have food. Take a seat."

Slocum and Harte took a table and Gloria hurried off, talking to someone in the kitchen as she disappeared.

"Good woman," Harte said. "Williams planned to arrest Worthington, but he cut out for Tucson and is hiding there behind some high-priced lawyers."

"No Gantry, no Worthington, huh?"

"Right. Aw, we'll get them all. The governor is appointing me as the interim sheriff. Oh, yes, and Searle Bakker was released today from Yuma and should be on his way here."

"Bet he's happy. I know that Bob will be."

Gloria brought their food. "Guess I could stay open night and day."

"You do have those two opening up in the morning, don't you?" Harte asked her.

"If they get up. Bet there's some hot coffee."

"We'll take it," Slocum said.

"Don't you worry, they'll be here all right." Harte shook his head as she left. "She's trying to cut back some on her hours. Since she came back, her business has been booming. Folks really missed her."

"I bet," Slocum said, about to decide that Harte had more than a passing interest in Gloria.

"She's a great woman," Harte said.

"She is."

"Oh, yes," Harte said. "I received a telegram sent to Gantry. Those folks in Kansas would not send any reward money to him for your arrest until their deputies had arrived and verified that it was really you he held in jail. I guess they've been skinned before?"

"And?"

"I'm sure not turning you over to them."

"Good." He went back to eating. "They say when they would be here?"

"No. Sounded like it would be a while. Why?"

"Then I still have some time to help tie this up."

Harte looked around the empty café before he whispered, "If you see the U.S. flag at half-mast over the jail, ride on."

"Thanks."

"By the way, how's my bay horse?"

"Worn out. You have a fresh one?"

"Sure do. Aren't you going to sleep?"

Slocum looked up at him before he took another bite of the tasty food. "I can sleep later. I want to check on the drilling. Then I may ride south and look for Gantry."

"You think you may know where he's at?"

"I'm going looking anyway."

Gloria came back in, wiping her shiny face on her apron,

and then stood beside Harte. He reached out and hugged her waist familiarly. "Can you believe Slocum is going back to Bob's place tonight?"

"I don't doubt it." She looked at Slocum. "Tell her hi."

Slocum put down his fork, too full to eat another bite. "Thanks to you two for supporting her. I don't think she'd ever have done it by herself."

"She's a brave girl and we understand you have to move on. Damn shame. She really talked a lot about you." Harte looked up at Gloria for verification.

"Jeff's right. Isn't there any way you can stay?"

"Thanks, but I better make tracks."

"Wait, I'll go with you." Harte scraped his chair on the floor.

Slocum reached over and put his hand on his shoulder. "I can trade horses myself down at the livery. You two can use some time together. If I don't see you again, the company's been great, the food was wonderful, and thanks."

Gloria smiled and winked at him as he shook hands with Harte and said, "You won't ever win the next election for sheriff if you make her close this café."

They both laughed.

Under the stars, he led the bay from the jail hitch rack to the stables. He woke the hostler and told him the sheriff had sent him to trade for another of his horses.

"Huh? Huh? Got a lot of nerve sending you down here in the middle of the night." Coughing interrupted his grumbling as he made his way with a lamp back in the barn to where two stout horses stood by themselves in a tie stall. The first one turned back to look at Slocum, and he caught the look in his eye.

"This one will do."

"High-priced dudes," the old man mumbled. "One you brought in looks wrung out."

"He is, but he's not hurt."

"Well, I'll look him over in the daylight."

"Fine," Slocum said, not interested in the old man's problems. He led the fresh horse out and quickly changed saddles. He put his kac on the chestnut horse, thanked the old man, and headed for the door.

"Wait, I'll bring the light."

"I'm fine," he said, nearly outside.

"What was your name so I can tell him who got his hoss?"

He stepped in the stirrup out under the stars. "Slocum." And he rode off.

At night, he wouldn't make a great target for that shooter whoever he was. The new bay threatened to buck. They went sideways up the dark street for a block. The bay danced on his toes. The whole time, Slocum patted his neck and tried to talk him out of breaking in two.

Who could that shooter be? He needed to solve that, too.

Chapter 17

Dawn gilded the far sawtooth range in gold. He came off the same ridge where he'd dropped his saddle that first morning. The chestnut gelding had earned his name, Big Man, by the time Slocum reined him up at the house.

"Slocum," Bob called out. "Coffee is on. I have some oatmeal ready. Come on in."

He hitched Big Man at the rack, loosened the girth, and went to the porch. She stood in the doorway, cradling a cup of coffee in her hands, as he washed up.

"Well, how is it going?" he asked.

She shook her head with mischief dancing in her eyes. "I never thought you'd come back to see me ever again."

"I'm here." He shrugged, drying his hand on a flour-sack towel.

She looked off to the north, then stepped back. "There's water running in the tank up there."

"You hit it?"

She nodded, biting her lower lip. "Haney says it needs to be opened up and we'll have lots of water."

"Your brother is on his way home."

"Oh, Slocum, won't he be excited about the water?"

"I'd say so. Where's Haney?"

157

"He and Dan went to Barlowville. There's some pipe up there at an abandoned mine that they think they can make a valve for to turn the water off and on."

She stepped back for him to enter and hung a hand on his shoulder. "I'm so glad that you came when we could be alone."

At the table, he put his hands on her waist. "So I guess you aren't committed to anyone."

"Committed to anyone. You tease." Her hands went around his neck and she kissed him.

"Do I have time to eat?"

"I may feed you."

"Good. Sit on my lap."

She let him sit down, then moved in. Wiggling herself in place, she filled a spoon with oatmeal. He leaned forward, hugging her, to take it off the spoon. Then chewing it slowly, he considered the buttons on her blouse. With his left hand, he reached in and unbuttoned them one at a time.

With his next mouthful ready for him on the spoon, she drew in her breath. "This may be hard."

"Hard?"

She blushed. "That, too."

He gently massaged her firm breasts, kissed the side of her face, and savored her closeness—the sweet lilac smell of her perfume. Eating oatmeal soon took second place. She straddled his lap and leaned back so he could feast on her rock-hard nipples. The world began to swirl. Her flesh tasted sweet and the whole thing was heady enough to make him dizzy.

Filled with a strong need for her, he swept her up and carried her to the fresh-made bed.

They scrambled to undress, not wanting the fire to diminish one flicker. Then they were on the bed skin to skin. With his rising erection between her legs, they dove into kissing. Her tight breasts were between them and that reminded him of their taste and condition. As they lay side by side, his hand ran over her pubic hair, and slid downward when she parted her legs for him. His middle finger soon probed her, and she moaned as he worked her slowly but surely.

Out of breath, she gasped. "Yes. Yes."

At her words, he moved over her and she bent her knees to give him access. His hard shaft eased into her and she clutched his forearms. With the back of her calves on his shoulders, he began to make hard thrusts in her tight pussy.

The faster he went, the louder she cried out. "Oh, yes. Oh, yes."

Sweat began to grease his belly from his efforts. His breath came in short gulps, and then two needles speared deep in his butt and he went to the bottom of her well.

Fire spewed out the head of his dick, and they collapsed.

"Oh, Slocum. I know this will be our last time, but I won't ever forget it. I swear I won't."

He put the side of his hand under her chin, raised her face, and then sipped honey from her mouth.

Then they dressed and he finished his cold oatmeal. Afterward, they rode up to the new well. Before he dismounted, he could see the liquid coming out was impressive.

"Haney says it'll do much better than that when he gets it open all the way. If they can make a valve to shut it off when I don't need the water."

"It'll be great. I come back next time, I want to smell alfalfa hay." He hugged her shoulder when she joined him.

"You will. I wish Daddy was here to see this happening. He'd sure have loved the notion."

"You're carrying on a great tradition. Searle will be here soon to help you finish the project."

"And Haney." She shook her head in defeat. "He's such a serious guy, but you were right—he's much more of a man than I first thought and he's smart."

"You three will build an empire."

She looked at the sky for help.

"I'm not kidding. And Harte likes the sheriff job enough, he never denied he'd run for the office when I teased him about Gloria."

"What about Gantry? Where's he?"

"Taking potshots at possible witnesses." Earlier, he'd told her about the ambush.

"You think it was him?"

Slocum nodded. "You keep an eye out."

"Oh, I will. Where are you going next?"

"Those Kansas deputies will be here in a day or so. I need to vanish. Harte can handle things with the deputy U.S. marshal and his own new crew. I figure that Gantry will show up and they'll arrest him."

"You know I won't forget you. Finding those doubloons and all you've done for us—for me."

"Hey, you loaned me a horse, remember?"

"Big deal." She feigned hitting him in the chest with her gloved fist. "You better ride out and now. I can't stand to be around you without thinking about doing it—again."

He agreed, kissed her quickly, and headed for Big Man. Mounted, he checked the powerful horse and waved to her—then he rode off. With a heavy heart, he short-loped the gelding. Hard to leave a real woman like Bob. Damn those deputies anyway . . .

By sundown, he was at Marie's crossroads store. In the twilight, he saw Smoothers come out on the porch with his arm in a sling.

"About time you came by," the man said.

Undoing his cinch at the hitch rail, Slocum laughed. "Cooking must be good around here."

"Hell, you should know, you sent me over here."

"I didn't figure you'd homestead."

"Aw, you two quit arguing," Marie said from the doorway. "Me and that Chinaman's hungry. Supper's on."

Slocum laughed at her as she stood in the doorway.

"Yes, ma'am, I'm coming." He swept off his hat and bowed.

"Well, wash up and then you can tell me what's happening," Smoothers said.

Seated at the table over supper, he told them all about Bob's well coming in, the new sheriff, Searle coming home, the ambush, Phelps in jail with the two rustlers, Worthington hiding out behind some lawyers in Tucson, and Gantry on the lam.

"And where are you headed?" Smoothers asked Slocum.

Marie passed Smoothers another buttered biscuit. She'd already cut up his meat for him. "Maybe he's just tired of all the trouble we've been having around here," she said.

"He probably is."

"It's time," Slocum said between bites.

"What do you think about the well?"

"I think I'd like to own a share in Haney Thorpe's well-drilling business."

"I may become his partner," Smoothers said.

"He could use you."

Lo looked over at them like they were crazy. "Have sawmill, now drill rig. You buy railroad next?"

"Where's one for sale?" Smoothers asked. They all laughed.

After the meal, he thanked Marie and shook Smoothers's good hand. She'd told them she had a buyer for the store and that she planned to continue his recuperation at Pine Canyon.

"He may never use it again," Slocum warned her.

"I thought about that, too."

He left them holding each other on the porch of the store, and rode on to Harte's place.

The moon was high when he dropped off the last ridge to the ranch. The pearly light shone on the oxbow in the line of dark cottonwoods. Big Man acted like he knew the place and was anxious to be back. The road was a switchback, and soon spilled him off on the flats and the alfalfa plots.

The night breeze stirred the cottonwoods enough to keep them spinning. He rode up to the hitch rail, looking about for Nevada and his rifle. No sign of him. Slocum dismounted, pulled down the crotch of his pants, and stood for a moment listening to the crickets.

Big Man snorted, and he unlaced the girth.

"Who's out there?" a woman asked.

"Slocum," he said.

"Slocum?"

"It ain't his brother."

Cora came down the walk in a long dress with a small lamp. "I really didn't expect you to ever come back—"

"Surprise, surprise. Where's Nevada?" he asked.

"You can stay?" she asked, putting her hand on his arm.

"I'm traveling through."

"Put him in the stables."

"Where's Nevada?"

"He's working some cattle. He'll be back in the morning. I'm fine."

He shook his head and scowled at her carelessness. "You don't need to be alone out here. Your brother hasn't caught Gantry yet."

"Good, then you can stay and guard me." She swung on his arm and the lamp waved about in her other hand, sending their shadows dancing in the night. "I feel much safer now."

"Gantry could be vicious if he gets his hands on you." He took the saddle off Big Man and put it on a rack. Then he turned him into a stall and slipped the bridle off.

When he hung the headstall and reins on the saddle horn, she blew out the lamp. "We don't need that anymore."

She set it down and then snuggled against him. "I am shocked you came back. I thought you'd never come back to me."

With a hard squeeze, she let go and then stood on her toes to kiss him.

"Now why would you ever think that?" he asked, then kissed away her answer.

When they finished, she held him around the waist. "You want a shower?"

"I could use one, unless you like the smell of horse."

"With you, I could stand a lot."

"Water warm?"

"Who cares?" She twirled around and came back to him. "I have you for a night or forever."

"Tonight."

"You can't tell, my web may keep you here."

"I can." They reached the shower area and he began to toe off his boots. She started to unbutton the dress's small buttons down the front. When his boots and socks were off, he shed his vest and the shirt, then his pants. Under the barrels, he looked at the two ropes. "Which one do I pull?"

Shrugging the dress off her shoulders in the starlight, she shook her head. "I'm not sure. Try one."

The cold spray felt icy on his head and he let go with a shiver.

"Sorry."

"I'll get even."

Her naked form looked like pearl in the moonlight and her blond hair looked silver when she reached the ring of the shower of water. Her hands moved over his body and when she knelt before him, he released the rope, stopping the shower.

The touch of her tongue made him want to stand on his toes. He closed his eyes as she worked on him. Then she took the head in her mouth and the edge of her teeth grazed the skin and made him more excited. Acting anxious to get him off, she jacked on him harder, then slipped it back in her oral cavity and sucked on it with all her might.

When he came, he pulled the wrong rope and the cold

water cascaded all over them. She fell on her butt, laughing.

"What a shocker."

He pulled her up and kissed her hard. "Sorry."

Then he used the other rope, and they were embraced in a warm shower as they held tight to each other, searching each other's mouth with a deepening need. Then they wadded up their clothes and hurried to the main house.

Inside, she bolted the door and they ran upstairs in the dim candlelight to her room. She dried her hair with a furious toweling, and he held her from behind by the waist. When she finished, she nestled her butt against him and threw her head back for him to graze on her neck and throat.

In the deep feather bed, they coupled and sought each other for a long time. She came several times. Then she began to contract inside and he felt her clit like a nail on the top of his stiff dick. And a volcano blew the end off the head of his manhood.

Exhausted and limp, they slept in each other's arms.

Chapter 18

"Señora! Señora!"

Cora bolted up in bed. "For God's sake, Juanita, what is wrong?"

"Three men are going through the buildings. They tried the front door, but I would not answer it," the girl said in a loud whisper from behind the door.

Cora looked over at Slocum, who was already pulling on his pants. "Who do you think it could be?"

She hustled into a robe and then let the girl inside her bedroom. "Do you know any of these men?"

"Would she recognize Gantry?" he asked.

Cora shook her head. "She's from Mexico. Do you think it's him?"

"Who else would be searching your buildings and trying to get in your house?" He checked the loads in his .44. "I thought he might be hiding at that abandoned place south of here where they held the Bakker girl."

"I have no idea. I met him twice. Never liked him. He was at some political meetings that Jeff took me to."

"You girls stay here and lock this door. You have a gun?"

Cora looked taken back. "I do."

"Use it if they try to get in. I mean shoot through the door."

"Can I help you?"

He shook his head. "I want you and her safe. Is there anyone else in the house?"

"The cook Maria," Cora said in a whisper to him as he stood beside the window trying to see where the men were standing.

"Get her up here, too."

"I'll go get her," Juanita said.

"No," Slocum said, not wanting them apart. "You go together and then you all barricade yourselves in here—take your gun, too."

Cora rushed back and got the pearl-handled pistol out of a dresser drawer. "What will they do to us?"

"Nothing," he said, leading the way out on the balcony. "Not if you shoot them first."

He saw no sign of anyone in the house, and led them to the kitchen. An older woman looked up in shock when he came in the room first.

"Come, Maria," Cora insisted, and the woman looked dismayed but obeyed, and the three went back up the stairs.

Slocum, revolver in his hand, saw a shadow pass the narrow barred kitchen window. He could hear grit grinding under the man's soles. Then the man tried the thick back door. His boot crashed against it—then his shoulder. Nothing gave. Slocum eased the latch, and when the man hit it again, the door opened. He fell inside and Slocum bashed him over the head. The man's pistol went spinning across the tile floor. Slocum closed and bolted the door, then tied the man's hands behind his back with his kerchief.

The invader looked unfamiliar to him. He dragged him by the collar into a pantry, stuck a sack towel in his mouth for a gag, and then bolted the door shut. He retrieved the pistol off the floor and stuck it in his waistband. Two guns wouldn't hurt.

Where were the others?

Suddenly, there was a rifle report and glass shattered upstairs. He turned an ear to listen.

"Surrender and come out now!"

Gantry—you sumbitch. Slocum began to breathe hard. There were only two of them left. He had to slip out and take them one at a time.

"Where's Yodder?" the other guy asked Gantry.

"Around back."

"No, I can't find him."

"He can't just disappear—"

He's in the pantry, stupid. Slocum slipped out the back door, taking the key ring off the wall. The door lock worked with the old key to lock position. Not as good as the bar or bolt, but at least it would stop them some if they went to beating at the door.

"Tell Yodder we need to empty our rifles in those upstairs windows."

"How can I? I can't find him."

"Well, maybe he's taking a shit."

"No, something's happened to him."

"Get around back and shoot the upstairs windows out."

Slocum hurried to the outhouse and slipped inside the bad-smelling interior. No, Yodder wasn't in there. He stood and listened to the fall of boot soles coming in his direction, then the click of a lever-action rifle. Each shot sent glass flying. One. Two. Three. Four. Five. Six. Clicked on empty.

Slocum slammed open the outhouse door and struck the man over the head. He wilted, his knees buckled, and he went down. Slocum jerked the rifle out of his hand.

"Carson, you reloading? Damnit, Carson." Gantry sounded uncertain. "Answer me, gawdamnit."

Slocum was bent over the unconscious man, shoving fresh rounds in the .44/40 magazine.

"Carson! Yodder!"

With the Winchester loaded, Slocum headed for the

front of the house in a long lope. He looked up in time to see Cora in the bedroom window cussing and blasting away with her pistol at someone in front of the house.

"Cora, get inside!" he ordered.

Hearing his words and holding the pistol in both hands, she disappeared inside.

When Slocum cleared the corner, he knew Gantry had already run for his horse. He ran harder, but a horse was getting away. He dropped to one knee and took aim at the fleeing horse and rider beyond the post-and-rail fence. Two quick shots and Gantry was gone out of range.

He wanted to rush to the barn, get a horse, and go after him, but he couldn't leave the two outlaws to the women.

"You all right?" Cora called down.

He waved. "I have one in the backyard to get and one in the pantry to round up."

"Pantry?"

"You can come downstairs. I'll be there in a minute or so."

The shooter out back was still on his butt, rubbing his head and wondering what devil had jumped out of the crapper and knocked him out. Slocum pulled him up to his feet.

"Where's your boss headed?"

"Huh?"

"You want your balls roasted?"

"No."

"Then tell me where Gantry's run off to."

"My head hurts. Damn, how should I know?"

" 'Cause there's an old Mexican woman in there going to cut your pecker off and then eat your balls raw if you don't—"

Maria had the door open and stuck her head out.

At the sight of her, the outlaw threw his arms over his face. "No. No. I'll tell you. It's some old ranch south of here."

"What is?" Cora demanded. Dressed in a riding outfit with her blond hair tied back with a ribbon, she came out and looked defiantly at the outlaw.

"Where Gantry's hiding." Slocum shoved the outlaw through the door into the kitchen. "Open that pantry door slow-like."

The gray-haired Maria's hand shook as she drew back the bolt. Then she stepped back as she opened the door. Hands over her mouth, she began to laugh and shake her head at the sight inside.

The other two women rushed over to peer at the outlaw seated on his butt with the towel stuffed in his mouth.

"Who are they?" Cora asked.

"Tell her."

The outlaw he had by the collar sullied.

"Maria, bring your biggest, sharpest knife over here."

The bug-eyed outlaw quickly swallowed and began to speak. "We was hired by Gantry to take you all prisoner and get them others out of jail in exchange."

"Where's Worthington?"

"I swear, I don't know him."

"What's your name?"

"Ed Carson and he's Frank Yodder."

"Jerk that gag out of his mouth," Slocum said.

Cora stepped in and when she took the gag away, the outlaw gasped for breath. "Who in the hell are you?"

"Slocum's my name. You heard of me?"

Cora steadied him to get him on his feet, and then she shoved him into the kitchen. "Do you two to know how much those windows you shot out will cost to replace?" she demanded.

"No, ma'am," Yodder said.

"Over a hundred dollars. How much money you got on you?" She held out her hand.

"We ain't got no money," Carson said.

"What shall we do with 'em?" She turned to Slocum.

"Send then to Antelope Springs for trial is all that I know."

"Makes me so mad. I'd personally horse-whip them."

"When's Nevada coming back?"

"This evening sometime."

"Good, he can take them up there. I'm sure Jeff will keep them for the judge."

"What're you going to do?" Cora asked.

"I'm going to track down Gantry after I tie them up and lock them in the tack room. Nevada can take them to jail when he returns."

"Maria, fix all of us some breakfast," Cora said with a displeased look at Slocum. "We can clean up the broken glass later."

"You two head for the shed," Slocum said. "Try anything and I'll cut you down in your tracks."

"I'm going with him," Cora announced, and marched beside Slocum behind the two outlaws.

"I guess you won't reconsider my offer?" she asked under her breath.

He shook his head. "You know it's not you. I've got men after me."

"I could hide you. No one would ever . . ."

"That's far enough. Carson, put both hands on that shed wall and lean out. You make a move, you're dead." He holstered his gun and took down some rope from the wall. It was stout enough hard hemp. He bound Carson's hands. Then he forced both men to lie on their bellies on the floor of the feed room and tied their feet together. Next he threw the end of the rope over a rafter to pull their knees off the floor a few inches, and tied it off. Then he strung another lariat under their armpits, and tied it to a post in the center so they were suspended between the posts and the rafter.

"Hell, we'll die like this," Carson said.

"I doubt it, but you'll sure be here dead or alive when her foreman gets back."

"You can't leave us in here to die," Yodder said before Slocum closed the door.

Slocum looked inside at them. "You would have raped

and killed those women in the house an hour ago. I ain't got any love for either of you."

Slocum closed the door and put a bolt in the hasp. "They should be there when Nevada returns."

"Will you come back and see me?" Cora clung to his arm as they went toward the house.

"You can find a better man."

"I don't want a better man. I want you. Can I come and join you sometime? I'd be very secretive."

"It's too dangerous, Cora."

"Am I what? Too fat? Too ugly? What is wrong with me?"

"It isn't you. It's me."

She stopped him short of the back door. "I have some money. I can meet you somewhere. No one will ever know about us. Do you trust me?"

He hugged her. "What I want and what I must do are two different things."

"Will you try it?"

He could smell her fine perfume. The rich sweetness intoxicated him. His eyes closed. He held her tight in his arms—eaten up about staying there and about going on. Cora was old enough, wise enough to know what she really wanted. He was, too. But his conscience said, *You can't.*

He minded his conscience a lot.

"If I find a place—I might write you."

She tossed her head back and then pushed the golden hair back from her face. "Don't might—write me. I promise not to bitch at you or complain about where it is at or how primitive a place it is. If it is only for a short while, I promise to be agreeable."

She clutched her hands together and beat him lightly on his breastbone. "Promise me."

"All right. If I find a place—"

She stood on her toes and kissed him. "I can wait. It won't be easy, but I can wait."

"If I find the opportunity, I'll write for you. The letter will come from Tom White."

The name tumbled off her lips. "Tom White. I'll be waiting." She hooked her arm in his. "You must eat breakfast now and promise me you will be careful. You can drop me a line now and then even if I can't come. I don't care if you don't write much. Like, 'I am fine. Tom White.' "

He nodded. He'd heard her.

Chapter 19

Over the next two days, he tracked Gantry's flight to Tucson. Gantry had ridden two good horses into the ground. Slocum found one of them at a ranch. The animal in question was down in the corral. The owner, a man named Henry, showed him the broken-down pony.

"I never allowed him much in trade for him," Henry said. "I may have to take him out and shoot him. Don't think he'll ever be any good."

The hip-shot horse hung his lead low and coughed in the dust. He was gaunt as a ghost and his hindquarters looked caved in. The saddle sores on his withers were raw and scabbed over. His coat was still white from sweating salt.

"What color horse did you trade him?"

"A ring-tailed bay. You can't miss it. Got a coon tail with bands of black and white. Good colt, young and green broke, but he never bucked much when your friend left out on him." Henry leaned back from the corral to look Slocum over. "Hell, I thought the devil hisself was after that man."

Slocum thanked Henry and rode on. The next day late in the afternoon, he found the ring-tailed bay in a wide, dry wash, bleeding out his nose, crusted in salt, with his eyes sunk in his head, saddle and bridle still on him. *Rode to death.* Slocum shot him in the center of the forehead with his .44 to put him out of his misery.

A few miles farther, he came to a ranch and store with a windmill creaking. He watered Big Man, who Cora had insisted he take with him, at the stone-mortar tank. A whiskered man came out in overalls, his pants tucked in knee-high boots. He took a corncob pipe out of his mouth.

"I'm looking for a man came through here on foot a while ago," Slocum said and dismounted. He loosened the cinch and then hitched Big Man to the rack.

"You're too late." The man had a rusty-sounding voice. "He done caught the mail wagon to Tucson a couple hours ago."

"Guess I'll find him there then."

"I ain't too sure. He looked like a man with his pants on fire." He used his pipe to point off in that direction. "He sure never wanted to see you again."

"He say that?"

"Nope. I jest figured it out when I seed you ride up. He's lost some growth, too, I'd bet."

"Maybe in prison he can catch up."

"What all did he do?"

"Murdered some, raped some, robbed some, and run a bad sheriff's office."

"Marthie," he said over his shoulder. "Fix this man some food. He's after that crazy guy walked in here this morning."

Skinny Marthie appeared in a wash-worn Mother Hubbard dress and smiled at him. Her front teeth were gone and she was cross-eyed, turning her head to the side to look at him. "I said he was no good and on the run. Lord, if I could see that, anyone could. Come in, mister, I's got vittles I can feed ya."

He nodded to the man and followed her inside the store, which was cluttered with dusty new overalls, bottles of patented medicine, cheap frying pans showing some rust, and a table of one-size-fits-all brogans. There was also an open tow sack of brown beans and crackers in tin cans that you could open and close.

She dipped him out some white ham bones and beans in a metal pot with a wire handle and handed it to him with a spoon. "Want some corn bread?"

He nodded, and she took a handful of dodgers out of a poke and put them on the table beside his pot. "That should fill you. Does most folks. Fact is, most can't eat it all."

He could believe her. Since he'd sat down, he'd noticed more flies in the place than a dead cow drew. Under the table, he shined the spoon on his pants, satisfied it had been recently washed. She was right, his appetite had slacked a lot.

"I need to get on to Tucson. How much do I owe you?"

"Ten cents."

He paid her, thanked her, and told the old man he'd see him again sometime and rode on. It was two hours later before he could even chew on some beef jerky from his saddlebags. A knot he couldn't swallow kept climbing up his throat.

The next day, he reached the Santa Cruz River about midday, and instead of riding into the town, he rode upstream to Louise Martinez's jacal. He didn't want to enter Tucson in broad daylight and broadcast his presence in the place.

An old wooden-wheeled *carreta* was parked in a bed of prickly pear. A white burro stood hip-shot by the house, sleeping and stomping at the biting flies without waking. Some fighting chickens scratched in the yard, and a long line of clothes hung on the line.

When Big Man snorted in the dust, a short Mexican woman came to the doorway to watch him dismount. Her dark eyes studied him hard; then a smile of recognition crossed her full lips.

"I have not seen you in a long time, my lover." She rushed out, skirt in hand, and hugged him. "It has been almost a year. Come in. Come in. Let me look at you. Oh, my, you have lost weight, too."

"I'm fine. Let me put my horse in your pen and feed him. Then we can talk about fun times, huh?"

"Oh, yes." And then she began to babble to him in Spanish about how long he'd been gone from her and how she had missed him every day. With her hip hard against his leg, she led him and the horse to the pen under the rustling cottonwoods. Slocum could smell the armload of rich sweet alfalfa she put in the manger for the horse.

"There is water, too, for him over there."

Slocum agreed and thanked her. Then he unsaddled the horse and put his rig on the pole fence. He'd be fine. So would the horse.

"I must go get some more wine," she told him.

"How long will you be gone?"

"Thirty minutes maybe."

"Good, I need a siesta."

She wrinkled her nose at him. "Sleep a lot. I have much work for you." Then she laughed at her own joke, and afterward acted embarrassed.

He gave her money for the wine and some meat. "Louise, see if you can learn anything about a man named Worthington. Where he stays. What he does each day."

She nodded and repeated the name.

"The second man's name is Gantry. He just arrived. He may be with the other man. I really need to know all about them. I would even pay someone to find them for me."

"I will see what I can learn." She looked at the money in her small hand and smiled at him. "We will have a great party."

He bent over and kissed her. From the doorway, he watched her hurry away. Then he toed off his boots, hung his six-gun holster on a chair nearby, and sprawled out in the hammock. Despite the afternoon heat, he was soon asleep.

"Wake up. Wake up. I have man that knows of this *Wordington.*"

He awoke—Louise was back. He swung his legs over the edge and rubbed his sleepy face.

"This is Lomas," she said about the man who stood before him dressed in the clothes of a peon. He held a great straw sombrero over his chest.

Slocum spoke to him in Spanish. "How are you today?"

"I am fine, Señor. She says you wish to know about this man Worthington."

Slocum nodded.

"He rents a small house here that he uses when he comes to Tucson."

"He comes often?"

"*Sí*, Senor. They say he is very rich."

"Can you draw me a map to this place?"

"*Sí*." The man dropped to his knees, and in the dirt floor drew a map with his knife. With the blade tip pointing at an intersection, he said, "This is La Huerta Cantina here."

Slocum nodded. He'd been there before.

"Go one block south. Turn west, it is the second house on the right."

"I can find that. Is this man Gantry here?"

"I don't know, Señor. Do you need him, too?"

"You have done very good." He paid him two pesos.

The man bowed his head twice. "She said you were a very generous man. *Gracias*." He left, still impressed with his pay.

Louise came over, put her arm around Slocum's neck, and slipped into his lap. "How long can this person wait?"

"Why?"

"'Cause I need you for a while." She pushed the hair back from his forehead.

"You may have me."

She wrinkled her nose. "I better feed—"

His mouth cut off her words. And when he began to kiss her, she hoisted her skirt to free her legs and sat straddling his lap. They kissed, and his hands molded her breasts under the blouse until she quickly shed it and grinned at him.

In no time, they were on the hammock. Her small body was folded in two with her feet on his shoulders and him poking her hard. Sweat greased his belly, and the drum of her heels on his collarbone sent him off into a faraway land and he came. They collapsed in the hammock.

"I must fix some food. There are people coming for fiesta."

He hugged her. "Who?"

"Good people. You know some of them."

He released her and she bounded off the hammock to quickly dress. "You know, I wish now I had invited no one to celebrate. We could have done that all night." Then she laughed. "We can still do it when they go home. Right, amigo?"

He agreed. She was like a bumblebee—buzzing all the time. He walked down to the river with a towel and soap and took a bath. No one stared at bathers. Women, children, even men used the stream. He saw no one this trip, but it was not uncommon to see a naked woman scrubbing her kids or washing her clothes in the buff.

The music soothed the night, and the Chinese lanterns illuminated the area in front of her house. A man brought a cooked side of calf. Others carried in dishes, and two women deftly made flour and corn tortillas like a factory.

Louise clung to his arm introducing him to people he'd met before and many he'd never met. They danced in the dirt—no ballroom needed. They danced fast and they danced slow.

A very pregnant young woman asked him to dance and when they were done, she made him bend down and then whispered in his ear, "There is room for you in there."

With her hand, she circled her bulging belly. "You won't hurt it."

"Maybe later," he said, and kissed her cheek.

Acting satisfied, she went waddling off. He was glad to be out of that situation, though he'd bet money she'd be a sweet lay. After a check of the stars, he went to find himself some food.

He slept in the next morning. When he awoke, he discovered that Louise had crawled into the hammock without any clothes on and was jacking him off. Needless to say, he had to finish that event.

"When will you go after this man?"

"When the sun goes down."

With a breast stuck in his chest and her on top, she pressed his hair back and looked him in the eye. "I don't wish to run you off."

"Someone coming?"

"No." She frowned black at him. "I mean, I don't want you to leave."

"I savvy, but Tucson is a bad place for me to stay very long. A big gringo in the barrio attracts too much attention."

"We are in the country."

"It's still part of it."

"Where will you go?"

He shrugged. "Away."

She wrinkled her nose. "You are a strange man, Slocum. You have a spell on me. I sleep with a man, I compare him to you. He never measures up. I can find no one better, so I take no one, huh? Then I hope you come back and see me again soon."

He smiled. Always, she was honest.

At dark, he made his way into Tucson. He found the cantina and then the house. There were lights on inside. Taking care, he circled it and from the alley, he slipped inside the adobe-walled yard. There was an open lit window, and he eased up to it to listen to the conversation he could barely hear.

"Damnit, Gantry, unless we break him out of that jail, he'll turn his guts inside out telling them everything."

"I missed killing him—"

"You've missed several things—Slocum getting out of jail—you should have killed him, too."

"Gawdamn it, Worthington. I did all I could."

"No, you haven't done it all."

"Why the gun—"

Two shots rang out and Slocum saw Gantry grab his guts and fall forward as gun smoke boiled out of the room.

"Why me . . ." Gantry gasped.

Coughing hard, Worthington came to the window to try and breathe. " 'Cause you no longer fit my plans."

Slocum found a uniformed policeman a block away. "There's been a murder."

"Who did it?"

"A man named Worthington. He shot the former sheriff of Saguaro County."

"Why did he do that?" They were both walking briskly in that direction.

" 'Cause they were in a crooked deal together that went wrong."

The policeman nodded. "Where is the body?"

"It was in the house a few minutes ago."

"Stay here," he said, and showed him that he wanted him to keep back. "I will go see about this matter."

"He shot him in the back room."

From across the dark street, he watched the policeman talk to Worthington in the lighted doorway. When Worthington refused him entrance, he insisted he had to look inside. They argued and the *policía* drew his pistol. He soon disappeared in the house.

Satisfied, Slocum smiled to himself, and then he turned on his heel to be lost in the night. Worthington would stand trial for murder—fancy lawyers might have trouble getting him out of that charge.

He went back to Louise's, toed off his boots, and shed his clothing. He found her asleep and naked on the shifting hammock. With his body nestled around her and a firm breast in his hand, he closed his eyes and went to sleep.

A cold north wind swept off the snowcapped mountains. In his sheepskin-lined jacket, he sat on the spring seat and drove the matched team in a jog. The town of Magdalena sat in a great basin surrounded by high peaks, and to the east it opened to the Rio Grande Valley. A skiff of snow from the night before had dusted the road and the sagebrush. The narrow tracks of the buckboard marked the white stuff as he dropped downhill toward the main rail cattle shipping point in New Mexico. The letter in his pocket read: *Dear Tom. I will arrive there on the eighteenth about three pm from my connection in Messillia. If you can believe those train schedules. Love, Cora.*

The sun offered little warmth, and he hoped she hadn't frozen to death in the passenger car coming over. He had several blankets for her to wrap herself in going back.

After confirming the possible arrival time in the depot, he went outside, sat in the buggy with a building blocking the wind, and waited. The train whistle ended his short nap, and he looked up to see the smoke churning out the stack as the train pulled up the grade to the depot

He stepped down and walked across the street. The porter was putting down the step and a couple of men in heavy overcoats came off next. Then he saw fringed shotgun chaps. She wore a man's leather coat. Her shoulder-length blond hair was under the new stiff white felt hat. Cora Harte had arrived in Magdalena.

He felt touched, and hurried over to hug her. On the platform, he swung her around and then kissed her. "I wondered if you'd even really come."

"Silly man."

"Well, we've got a long ride."

"Tell me about this cabin," she said, clutching his arm.

"You worried and want to go back?"

"Of course not. I make a deal, I keep a deal, Tom White," He set her down and took her luggage from the porter and tipped him.

The black man thanked him for the tip and said, "I bet Mrs. White, she sure be glad to be here."

"Yes, sir." Slocum looked at her standing beside the buckboard. "I bet she sure will be happy."

He wanted to sail his hat a mile. When her suitcases were in the back, he helped her up on the seat, and then he went around to get on the other side. The engine gave a loud whistle, released the air brakes in a hiss of steam, and began chugging out of the depot backward. It was the end of the line.

With a cluck to the team, they were headed back, too— to Tom White's snug cabin.

Watch for

SLOCUM AND THE BANDIT DURANGO

358th novel in the exciting SLOCUM series
from Jove

Coming in December!

And don't miss

SLOCUM AND THE TOWN KILLERS

Slocum Giant Edition 2008

Available from Jove in December!

DON'T MISS A YEAR OF

Slocum Giant
by
Jake Logan

Slocum Giant 2004:
Slocum in the Secret Service

Slocum Giant 2005:
Slocum and the Larcenous Lady

Slocum Giant 2006:
Slocum and the Hanging Horse

Slocum Giant 2007:
Slocum and the Celestial Bones

Slocum Giant 2008:
Slocum and the Town Killers

penguin.com

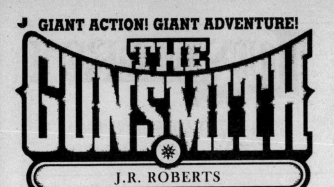

GIANT ACTION! GIANT ADVENTURE!

THE GUNSMITH

J.R. ROBERTS

Little Sureshot And
The Wild West Show
(Gunsmith Giant #9)

Dead Weight
(Gunsmith Giant #10)

Red Mountain
(Gunsmith Giant #11)

The Knights of Misery
(Gunsmith Giant #12)

The Marshal from Paris
(Gunsmith Giant #13)

penguin.com

M228AS0608

LONGARM

GIANT-SIZED ADVENTURE FROM AVENGING ANGEL LONGARM.

BY TABOR EVANS

2006 Giant Edition:

LONGARM AND THE OUTLAW EMPRESS

2007 Giant Edition:

LONGARM AND THE GOLDEN EAGLE SHOOT-OUT

2008 Giant Edition:

LONGARM AND THE VALLEY OF SKULLS

penguin.com

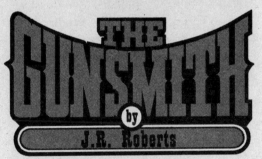